M000312250

My Escape from the Auto de Fé at Valladolid
October 1559

My Escape from the Auto de Fé at Valladolid
October 1559

Don Fernando de la Mina

A story founded on historic fact
and retold by Pastor Wm. Timms

Originally published in London by the Protestant Truth Society

*My Escape from the Auto de Fé at Valladolid
October 1559*

All rights reserved. This book may not be reproduced, stored in a retrieval system, or transmitted in any form or by any means, except for brief quotations in printed reviews, without the prior written consent of Zeezok Publishing.

ISBN 978-1-61006-110-0
Copyright © 2012 by Asociación Cultural y Estudiantil ICHTUS

Zeezok Publishing, LLC
PO Box 1960 • Elyria, OH 44036
info@Zeezok.com • 1-800-749-1681

www.Zeezok.com

Contents

Preface

It is our pleasure through the Salamanca based Christian-culture association ICHTUS to present this current edition of one of Protestant Spain's crown jewels in the historical-fiction genre of literature. You'll find a fun, surprising and intriguing story in these pages about Fernando de la Mina, a Spanish nobleman from Simancas, a town in the Castilian province of Valladolid near its capital city of the same name. Yet one of the most valuable virtues of this small volume is its ability to place you accurately in the exact geographic-historical-cultural setting of one of the stages of the ruthless annihilation of Protestantism from Spanish soil. In its unique narrative fashion you'll not only experience true-to-life examples of God's providence in the life of his children, but also acquire a real feel for what life was like as a Bible-believing Christian under the ominous cloud of the heretic-hunting Holy Office of the Inquisition.

As I first read this story I was immediately captivated by its trance since it held so many features of any cliff-hanging spy-thriller. Although I had studied different Spanish personalities that had risen to fame as they valiantly fought for freedom of conscious and open religious dialogue, Don Fernando helped me put flesh and blood on these figures and feel the fear as the unstoppable captain of the inquisitorial hounds flushed out the three fugitives from their hiding places barely avoiding the Church's clutches, representing the role of authentic Christianity in an age of radical cleric pharisaism. It was a bit of a personal epiphany, a reincarnation of sorts in which I could feel myself clothed with the rags of an itinerant peddler desperately racing against the odds, and facing the impossible task of concealing his identity even before the one he loved the most.

"My Escape" is quite an amalgam of different literary styles and techniques, embracing the first-person chivalry of a bourgeois nobleman who maintains a naive innocence concerning the nature of the Lutheran Reformation and the natural reaction of the hegemonic Roman Catholic Church of the 16th century, grossly underestimating her fury towards heretical impurity. Yet as sincere as Fernando proves himself, he soon discovers that through a set of providential circumstances he has been spared the most reprehensible and agonizing executions known to man, and must through extreme guile, cleverness and sheer shrew mark a new pathway of escape with a host of new disguises reminiscent of Peter Sellers in the Pink Panther. This new donquijotic protagonist now entertains us with hitherto unknown prowess and comic genius in order to reach the next town on his quest for liberation, security and religious freedom. One could almost expect it have begun, "In some place of (Castle) whose place I prefer not to remember, lived a noble gentleman named (Fernando de la Mina) . . . ."[1] The manner in which he fatefully falls into historic crucibles and momentous events such as the Massacre of Bartholemew's Day is reminiscent of Forrest Gump's penchant for being in key places at key crossroads of American history. There are also the cat and mouse chase scenes with the plump little monk that created hilarious images of Laurel & Hardy humor for me. How often the Bourne Trilogy of films also race through my mind as I envisioned a medieval fugitive of justice fighting for right but perplexed by his former friends having now become staunch enemies of the Truth. The tender and gripping romance between Fernando and Rosa entwined throughout the pages helps preserve the human and sentimental side to dogma, ceremony and tradition in perspective. When will Fernando finally reveal his true identity as the only rightful courtier

---

1   *This is similar to the very famous first line of the classic Spanish novel by Miguel de Cervantes entitled* The Ingenious Gentleman Don Quixote of La Mancha *(Spanish: El ingenioso hidalgo don Quijote de la Mancha), 1605.*

of this unrequited noble princess? What will she decide unmercifully cast upon the horns of a moral dilemma—to follow her conscience and the adventurous whims of an eccentric bohemian traveling mate, or to give in to the inertia of tradition and status quo. Oh the emotion when her Solomon finally reveals himself to his Sulamite maid as in the sapient song of Israel's wisest reagent! Such tension, such emotion, such dread, such horror, all in so few pages. Believe me, "My Escape" will leave you holding your breath to the very end.

I actually discovered this delightful volume on the Internet as I was doing research for my doctoral dissertation in Ibero-american anthropology through the University of Salamanca. It had been printed by at least three different publishing companies before, but apparently with limited readership and restricted popularity, even among students of the Spanish Inquisition. I was amazed that such an absorbing and fun love story could so eloquently be set against the fanaticism of 16th century Catholicism, and at the same time could be so strikingly contrasted with providence and biblical Christianity. The author's noteworthy writing style and extensive knowledge of Northern Spain so historically and geographically accurate drove me to a personal passion to have as many people read it, evangelical or not, historians or not, Spanish or not. From there I began to investigate about a Spanish version and discovered that none existed. I consulted with authorities on protestant history and only one pastor/writer had ever heard of the book. After tracking down the original publisher and attempting to identify the original author or first publication I came up empty handed. Since my search on copyright issues proved it was in the public domain, I began a search for a Spanish editorial house that would be interested in its publication. As a result, Demetrio Cánovas of Editorial Peregrino (Ciudad Real) became a good friend and soldier-at-arms in our endevour to get a Spanish edition out of the starting blocks.

My wife Belén and I spent several weeks translating a rough-draft, then our dear friend and award-winning poet Alfredo Pérez Alencart along with his wife Jacqueline fell in love with the book and offered to give it a face-lift. To be truthful, the text that Alfredo & Jacqueline returned to us bears as much resemblance to our first translation as a Velasquez painting does to fifth-grader's drawing, but after several months of hard work by the good folks at Peregrino we finally received the first copies in Spanish titled *Mi huída del Auto de fe de Valladolid* coinciding providentially, as Fernando de Mina would easily recognize, with the 450th anniversary of the Authos de Fe in Valladolid, both on the 21st of May and the 8th of October of 1559. The Spanish version has sold over 1,000 copies and has enchanted the evangelical readership of Spain's Christians as well as those in Hispanic-America. If anyone should wish to order a copy of the Spanish edition they can find it at: www.editorialperegrino.com. We are so grateful that Zeezok Publishing, LLC (www.Zeezok.com) has been willing to help us with layout, design and all of our printing expectations. We are especially grateful to Kris Wilcox, his kind suggestions and gentle encouragement. Scott Fulks did a lot of the leg work towards us reaching publication, his wife Juli coordinated the transcription process and Lorena Templeton did a fine job of creating an attractive cover.

But who is the *author* of this sensational story? We wish we could tell you but we can't. After as thorough an investigation as possible, our most educated conjecture is that is was Pastor WM. Timms in the late nineteenth or early twentieth century. Nothing is known of this pastor however, not even by the original publishers, the Protestant Truth Society of London. In all likelihood it was such a clergyman who also had traveled extensively in Spain and was not only well versed in her tortured evangelical past, but also in numerous details of medieval Spanish life, customs, geography and nomenclature. It does not appear to have been originally written in Spanish since there are no indications that a previous Castilian version existed before our own in 2010. This kind of apologetic protestant literature would not have been allowed press time or shelf space until the last two decades of the Twentieth Century, in any case. Another in the long line of curious enigmas this novel presents is how it has escaped the radar of so many Christian missionaries and workers in Spain. Very few of those I have had the privilege to know have heard the title; all of which, in a united whole, contributes to the aura of mystery that surrounding this anonymous tome that portrays with such excellence and imagery the barbarity of religious hatred and intolerance as well as the rays of hope that Reformation truthes brought to anxious souls. "My Escape" helps us all set the record straight, and reminds us once again of the enormous abyss between the Gospel message and the masses of Spaniards still trapped in their majority by the staunch momentum of the Catholic Church's culturally perpetuating machinery.

And what shall we say about the Inquisition that has not already been written in hundreds of volumes? The Holy Office of the Roman church in all of its respective countries reaching to the Americas was infamous in its tenacity to hunt down even the remotest suggestion of Lutheran, Jewish or Islamic heresy. Innocently called in prosaic latin *Inquisitio Haereticae Pravitatis* (an inquiry into heretic perversity), it began in the 12th Century as a movement to purify doctrine within the church. It ended in most countries after cruelly imprisoning, shaming, trying and processing thousands of people guilty or not, Catholic or not, through the sheer strength of its authoritative rule stretching across several internal institutions. Over 900,000 people in Europe alone were executed by her henchmen, nearly 30,000 in a weeks-long span of blood-thirsty rage during the St. Bartholomew Day Massacre in France, starting on August 23rd, 1572. Europe would soon enough forget such barbarity and massive genocide during the holocaust of the Jews in Nazi Europe, but our author calls us through this captivating story to never forget either one.

King Ferdinand II of Aragon and Queen Isabella I of Castile established the Spanish Inquisition in 1478. It was extended to all Spanish colonies and territories, which included the Canary Islands, the Spanish Netherlands, the Kingdom of Naples, and all of her possessions in North, Central, and South America. Phillip II, as our story tells us, was the fiercest persecutor of Protestantism and even claimed he'd light the torch to burn his own son at the stake if he embraced Reformation heresy! The Holy Office in Spain was officially closed in 1834, although in Italy it has never closed. It did however change its name to the "Congregation of the Holy Office of the Inquisition" in 1542 by Pope Paul III, in 1908 to "The Sacred Congregation of the Holy Office", and in turn to the "Congregation for the Doctrine of the Faith" in 1965. Curiously the last director of this department, until accepting a new assignment, was Joseph Aloisius Ratzinger, the current Pope Benedict XVI. The stale, cold facts of the sinister crimes of the Inquisition have mostly passed with impunity and exception, though the blood of so many martyrs still cries out from their ashen graves. Don Fernando, his beloved Rosa and her maid help us flesh out the factual experiences of so many of their counterparts in reality. Arguably the most famous case tried by the Roman Inquisition involved Galileo in 1633, when the "Father of Modern Science" was charged with such heretical and anti-Catholic ideas as the heliocentric nature of the solar system.

The *Auto de Fe* (literally "act of faith" or declaration of allegiance to Catholic dogma) that Fernando de la Mina witnesses and from which is providentially delivered was the ritual of the public trial and penance of condemned heretics and apostates that took place when the Inquisition had decided the appropriate punishment for their "crimes". It was normally followed by an execution effected by the civil authorities according to the sentences imposed. In this way both the Altar and the Throne participated in concert, similar to the kangaroo courts Jesus was subjected too. Just as the Romans then effected the crucifixions, it was the (un)civil authorities in Spain that actually carried out the burnings. The *hoguera* (or "burning stake") was just one of the instruments used to impose fear and exact confessions used by the Holy Office. The wide range of tools of torture used in this period are well known were designed to "convince" the accused of the orthodoxy of the Catholic religion. The accused were never allowed to face their accusers so that these "courts" more resembled vigilante justice that serious tribunals of law. Since execution by burning was more memorable than the penance which preceded it, the term *auto de fé* in popular use came to mean the burning rather than the penance. The stirring and poignant, although dated Bob Jones Unusual Films dramatization "A Flame in the Wind" (1971) well depicts the pomp, ceremony and relgious fervor of the Autos de Fe in Seville (the most famous of which was in 1560) where the convent of San Ildefonso was raided. This was the same convent from which a dozen or so Jeronymite monks escaped to exile, two of which translated and revised Spanish the first Bible in Spanish. Numerous Autos de Fe were held in various Spanish cities, normal regional capitals. In 16th Century Seville alone there were inquisitorial trials in 1524, 1546, 1559, 1560, 1562, 1570, 1571, 1573, 1574, 1575, 1578, 1579, 1580, 1586, 1592, 1596 and 1599.

Though published nearly a century later in Spain, the most famous Inquisition novel called *The Heretic* by Miguel Delibes (*El hereje*, first published in Spanish in 1998) has generated renewed interest in the persecution of Protestants, especially given the notoriety of Delibes as a well-known & prized writer & journalist who heretofore shared no special sympathies with Spanish evangelicals. It was also his last novel as he died in 2010. There are remarkable similarities between the Delibes' work and "My Escape" since both of them describe created personalities who experience the enchantment of the Scriptures, the rush of cryptic discovery and the dread of being publicly shamed, tortured and exececuted. Delibes' principal protagonist Cipriano Salcedo suffers a much more ignominious end than Don Fernando, but the novelesque treatment of 16th century Valladolid and the Auto de Fe of 1559 are no less accurate. Perhaps Cipriano's name was drawn from Cipriano de Valera, the first editor in 1604 of Casiodoro de la Reina's monumental translation into Spanish of the full Bible, first published in Basil in 1569.

Other novels in this growing genre of historical fiction about Spanish protestants include new publications of *Recuerdos de Antaño* (Memories from the Past) by Emilio Martínez (2009, CECyL), *El Libro de las memorias de las cosas* (The Book of the Memory of Things) by Jesús Fernández Santos (2012, Catedra) and *Los papeles del abuelo* (Grandfather's papers) by Febe Jordá (2009, Noufront). It is the hope and desire of the ICHTUS Cultural Association that this work even be carried to the Seventh Art and developed into a major movie production.

Without further adieu, the members and associates of ICHTUS invite you to an entertaining and educational evening of enjoyable, rapturous reading. We trust that you'll not allow your curiosity concerning events, names and places to go unrequited, but will be motivated to learn more about Spain's present by better understanding her past. Please, as you read, remember that the people in the nine provinces of Northwest Spain called *Castilla y León* still suffer from the enormous atrocity of having their only voices for Christ completely squelched by the flames of Valladolid, its first evangelical congregation totally annihilated. This first "church", after losing most of its members to the stake, even suffered the indignity of rock salt being scattered upon the ground where once stood the home of Dr. Augustin Cazalla, the first protestant pastor in Castile, after it was burned and razed by the "real" captains of the inquisitorial guards. Over three centuries would pass before anyone else with a true Christian heart would step foot on this soil. The Bible agent and "colportor" George Borrow sent by the British and Foreign Bible Society made a furtive pass through the Castilian country side and its principal cities during his journeys between 1936-40 (expertly elucidated by his famous book *The Bible in Spain*, first published in 1843). But even by 1886 there were only ten evangelical churches in all of Castilla y León, none in Segovia or Soria. Though there are over 220 churches in the region now, nearly half of these are gypsy churches that have little cultural relationship with the rest of Spain's residents. Most of these churches hold 30 attendees on average making it difficult to imagine even 15,000 people attending protestant churches in the largest geographic region in Spain, now home to four million people.

Some have speculated that there must be a divine cause to the spiritual barrenness in Spain, that she as a nation suffers a kind of theocratic curse for having expelled the Sephardic Jews in 1492, for having persecuted, tortured and callously executed Bible-believing Christians during the Counter-reformation, o for the marginalization and criminalization of evangelical believers during the dictatorship of General Francisco Franco. We're neither arguing for or against this claim, which could easily apply to any number of other countries in the world. But by the publication of this small glimpse into the injustices perpetrated by Catholic intolerance in Spain, we wish to promote a more religiously plural vision for this Iberian patria, home to an increasing number of protestant Christians. We wish to invite you to pray for souls held in religious and idolatrous darkness for too many centuries, and to implore that you pray that God would send forth more "labourers into his harvest" (Luke 10:2) to help us evangelize the "least-evangelized Spanish-speaking country", the cultural and linguistic fountainhead of the Hispanic world, yet the one country that has the fewest believing Christians than any of her daughter nations worldwide.

Should you have any questions about this book, request extra copies, or learn more about the ICHTUS Cultural Association in Salamanca, Spain, please do not hesitate to contact us at:

Kent B. Albright
President of the Asociación Cultural y Estudiantil ICHTUS
Nº de CyL: 3589, CIF: G37466679
Asn. insctª. USAL, Ayto. Salam. nº 621
ichtus.salamanca@gmail.com
www.ICHTUSalamanca.org
34-627-95-92-28

Introduction

In the afternoon of November 24, 1602, an attorney sat in the oak-panelled dining room of a merchant prince's London House, and there, in the presence of the heir and his friends, the attorney read the following will:

London, September 14th, 1601: I, Fernando de la Mina, Embroiderer by Appointment to Her Majesty, at the sign of 'The Golden Cross' on Cornhill in the City of London, do hereby bequeath to my son, Fernando de la Mina, my business and all my possessions together with the accompanying sealed document.

This sealed document was handed to the heir who, when he had read its startling superscription, placed it carefully inside his doublet in reserve for private reading. In the evening when his company had departed and young Fernando sat alone by his bedroom fireside, he once more read the superscription of the bequeathed document and read as follows: "A faithful record of my Providential Escape from the Torture and Fire of the Inquisition at Valladolid in the year of Our Lord 1559". With very few deletions and modernisings, this ancient manuscript read as follows:–

Chapter 1
My Arrest at Simancas

I Don Fernando de la Mina, a nobleman of Spain, was born on April 16, 1534, near Simancas—an ancient city which lies ten miles to the south of Valladolid, the capital of Spain. My mother gave her life for me when I was born and my father gave his life for his King and Country at the glorious victory of San Quentin. Thus, at the age of twenty-three years, I became the head of our ancient family and the owner of the Castillete de la Mina and the fourteen surrounding farms that constituted our family estate. Thereupon, early in September 1557, while the King was fighting in France, I was presented at the Regent Joanna's Court at El Escorial and there took the Oath of Allegiance to my Sovereign Lord, King Phillip the Second, whom may God rest. From that time until my twenty-fifth birthday I devoted my attention to our estate and the days passed pleasantly and profitably until the evening of April 16, 1559 (my twenty-fifth birthday), when a sudden catastrophe overwhelmed me in anxiety, poverty, and privation. I was at home that evening entertaining my friends at a supper party when, without a word of warning, four officers of the Holy Inquisition entered the hall and peremptorily forbade us to move from our seats until they had searched the Castillete for evidence of heresy.

Unwelcome visitations such as this were common enough in those days. It was no unusual occurrence for the homes of wealthy folk to be suddenly searched for heretical books. The servants, too, were often terrorized or bribed to betray their master's religious views and practices; and such betrayals of trust frequently involved their master's arrest, the confiscation of his property, torture, and death.

The reformed religious doctrines were then fast filtering into Spain from England, the Netherlands, and Germany. The dark ages of Medievalism were passing away, and the dawn of a New Truth was breaking upon the world—a Truth that challenged the time-long teaching and authority of the Church of Rome.

In consequence of the rapid spread of this new Lutheran teaching, the prelates of Spain became alarmed, and their alarm spurred them to violent acts of oppression. By means of the prison, the thumbscrew and the rack, they sought to prevent the people from learning and accepting the Reformed Christian Doctrines. They instituted priestly questionings at the enforced Confessional and sent their secret spies, disguised as servants, into the households of suspected folk. Tribunals were set up in every district to hunt out and arraign heretics. The unfortunate suspects were arrested and tortured, their property confiscated and their family names made infamous, and finally, if they remained staunch and unrelenting, they were publicly brought to trial at the Auto de Fé (the Act of Faith!) and there forced either to recant their heresy, or perish in the flames!

I searched my mind, in vain, to discover the reason for this untimely and unwelcome visit of the search officers of the Holy Inquisition. Had any of my neighbors or acquaintances denounced me to the Holy Office, thought I? Surely not, for I had not an enemy in the world, save, perhaps, Father Lorenzo, a very distant relative of mine. Did the Holy Office covet my estate and seek a reason to confiscate it? Perhaps!

But I had no fear, for I knew that the only evidence of my sympathy with the Reformed Faith were just a few books that lay discreetly hidden in the wall-recess behind my bed. Just a few Lutheran books in Latin and the four Gospels in Greek. These had been given to me on my previous birthday by the Doña Rosa de Riello—your mother, an orphan like myself and to whom I was then betrothed. The Riello estates joined mine, and your mother and I had fondly hoped that our marriage in the following May would prove a happy and a blessed union of body, soul, and estate. Our mutual love was sincere and beautiful. Our religious beliefs were similarly liberated and enlightened by the new learning and by the Gospels, which revealed the open Way to God and exposed the superstitions of the Roman Church and the pretensions of its misguided priesthood.

The searchers of the Holy Office quickly distributed themselves in the hall, and there they thoroughly ransacked every coffer and receptacle. Then they passed into my little cabinet (my workroom) that led into the *patio*, i.e., the large open courtyard in the center of the Castillete. But, failing to discover any heretical documents among my private papers, they then proceeded to the servant's quarters at the further end of the courtyard and from thence went up the stairs and round the gallery to the many sleeping chambers. But I, fearing nothing from the search, refused to allow the intrusion to interrupt on gaiety and I confidently encouraged my friends in cheerful conversation—and the wine and the laughter went merrily round!

But alas! How foolishly I had underestimated the vigilance of the searching officers! In less than twenty minutes, the Captain returned to the supper room carrying the incriminating books!

Our merriment immediately subsided. My companions, one by one, rose contemptuously from the table. The taint of heresy was upon me! I was discovered to be a traitor to my Church and Country!

One by one my erstwhile friends departed coldly and unceremoniously, and I was left alone "despised and reject"—a prisoner in the hands of the dread Inquisition. And, within half an hour of the arrival of the search party, I left my ancestral home—never again to enter its hospitable walls.

Chapter 2
Torture and Escape

A t the Captain's command, I at once left the banqueting hall and walked out from the Castillete with the officer along the familiar chestnut avenue toward the stables. But as we drew near to the angle of the farmhouse road I turned and took, what proved to be, my last farewell of the beloved home of my childhood— that stately Castillete de la Mina that had been our family possession ever since the proud day when Queen Isabella transferred it from Abn Eber, the vanquished Moor, and bestowed it on my great, great-grandfather as a rich reward for his generous and valiant service to the State—Oh, my son, if ever it shall be within your power to recover possession of our family estate, I pray you spare no labor or expense. Nevertheless I urge you not to compromise with your conscience— no! Not even for such a tempting earthly joy as the Castillete de la Mina, near the city of Simancas!

"Your Excellency," said the Captain as he courteously stepped aside, so that I might precede him into the stables—"Your Excellency will please instruct the stableman to ride upon one of my own horses" and dressed as I was in gala costume—the irony of it!—I was escorted as a prisoner along the roadway to Valladolid and there incarcerated in the prison of the Inquisition. No question was asked me, no judicial examination was made. I was, at once, placed in a small cell upon the first floor, the grated window of which gave out upon the dismal courtyard below. But, saving the restraint and loneliness under which I chafed, my first five months of imprisonment were not severe, for permission was granted that my food and extra might be sent to me from the Castillete de la Mina.

On the fourth or fifth of September, however, I was awakened at midnight and arraigned before the dread Tribunal in the vault of the prison!

Numbed with the cold and frozen with the horror of the scene, I shuddered with weakness and fear as I peered into the cruel eyes of the unknown Inquisitors, who glared upon me through the holes in their hooded masks. Three times they repeated their question before I understood its true significance.

"From whom," they demanded, "from whom did you receive the heretical books?"

There was but one answer to that question—it was silence, and a terrible retribution was dealt on me for that silence.

My son, do you remember how, as a little boy, you often inquired of me concerning the ugly swelled bones that disfigure my ankles and wrists and which always pain me so in damp weather? Oh God! That priestly men professing gentleness and love and charity could ever be so pitiless and brutal in their lust of wealth and power!

That night they tortured me upon the rack with ever increasing severity until, at last, all sense of suffering was providentially withheld from me in a merciful unconsciousness. Twice again they tortured me, and twice again a saving insensibility was providentially interposed.

The memory of those excruciating hours haunted me throughout the rest of my life!

For three weeks I lay upon my bed in constant pain, unable to stand or raise my arms, and it was not until the end of September that I was able to dress myself.

Early in the afternoon of Saturday, October 7, I was visited by the jailor, who treated me with gross indignity. He commanded me to descend into the courtyard and there assist the prison carpenters to complete the seven coffins that were required for the bodies of heretics who had recently died in jail, in order that their remains might be placed in them and burned tomorrow at the Auto de Fé! These coffins were painted with flames and devils in red and yellow, and it was my odious task—I, a nobleman of Spain!—it was my odious task to paint those hellish symbols on those coffins!

Now, my son, you may or you may not believe in special interventions of Providence. For my part, I believe in Almighty God, and I believe Him to be able and willing, at His own chosen time, so to control and direct the administration of His own irrevocable laws that the powers of nature shall work for the special well-being of His children. Listen!

No sooner had I descended into the courtyard and commenced my loathsome task than a great heat and lowering darkness descended upon us, and a terrific thunderstorm, such as you never experience in Britain's favoured land, broke over the city. The lightning flashed and crackled like brittle steel, and the earth swayed and shook under the savage roll of thunder. The carpenters, mad with fright, fled into the cellars. The keeper of the gate rushed into his lodge and stood there, blinded and gibbering as if he were struck with sudden madness!

In that moment of blackness and horror I crept to the gate, unbolted it, and passed, unobserved, through the little wicket into the narrow street outside. Swiftly I sped on in the darkness towards the river and there, spurred by fear and heedless of the danger, I leapt across the stream from stone to stone, just in time before the oncoming storm-flood began to sweep down in a wild, roaring torrent from the surrounding hills.

Chapter 3
In the Church of Arroya de la Encomienda

For two miles I ran on steadily along the Tordesillas road until I reached the Church of Arroya de la Encomienda. But there I could proceed no further because, by that time, the storm had begun to break forth again with renewed fury. One moment the whole country was enshrouded in blackness and the next moment it glittered with a blinding lurid light. Then again the darkness and the deluge fell, and it seemed as though the pent-up vengeance of Hell was let loose upon the trembling earth.

Exhausted and afraid I crept into the porch of the church and passed into the deserted sanctuary. "Deserted," did I say? No, it was not deserted, for, as I entered, I stumbled over something in the darkness. I reached down to discover what it was, and at that moment a vivid flash of lightning lit up the church and revealed there, lying at my feet—stark and ghastly—the distorted body of a poor *buhonero* (peddler). He had evidently met his death while seeking safety in that sacred edifice! The upper part of his face was burned beyond recognition. His *buhoneria* (peddler's box) lay overturned beside him and his paltry merchandise was scattered far upon the marble pavement. For some moments I stood paralyzed with horror. Then, gradually, the fear of recapture stirred my senses once more, and I began to perceive in this dreadful circumstance a providential opportunity of escape from my relentless pursuers. Quickly I stripped the peddler—no difficult task, for his complete attire consisted only of a course shirt, woolen breeches, a Moorish headkerchief, a black sombrero, a pair of clumsy shoes, and rag bandages in lieu of hose upon his feet. His hair and beard, like mine, were long and unkempt, and his skin was filthy, as mine had become through suffering and neglect. Quickly I stripped myself and then, garment by garment, I dressed the poor corpse in my birthday hose, my silken undervest with our family insignia embroidered at the neck, my silk and velvet doublet, and my shoes with gilded buckles. Then I forced upon his finger the costly purple topaz ring that King Phillip had presented to my father, and I left two gold pieces in the purse that I pressed into his doublet and retained the remaining five gold pieces for my own future emergencies. Then I clothed myself in the peddler's filthy shirt and breeches, his rags and shoes. I tied the frowsy kerchief round my head and donned his battered hat. I gathered up his scattered merchandise into the *buhoneria*, and, strapping the *buhoneria* to my waist, I knelt in thanksgiving to Almighty God for His most wondrous mercy toward me.

With a glad and grateful heart I rose, and, there and then in obedience to the Divine Will, I surrendered forever my proud family title and my heritage (but not my honour nor my faith in God), and leaving there upon that sacred floor the ghastly effigy of my dead self for the confusion and satisfaction of my pursuers, I turned to leave the church.

But just as I was about to pass into the porch four men entered, and I found myself surrounded by the officers of the dread Inquisition! I had evidently been seen running along the road, and the officers of the Inquisition had overtaken me. The Captain of the company was he who had arrested me at the Castillete de la Mina six months before! Did he recognize me now in the guise of a poor *buhonero*? No, thank God, for when he had espied and carefully inspected the gaily attired corpse that lay near by, he turned and brusquely bade me "Sirrah! Go and fetch your mule in from the roadside." That unexpected command was a fortunate one for me, for until then I did not know that I (or rather the poor dead *buhonero*) possessed such a luxury as a mule, and my ignorance of that fact might have cost me my life. So I went out and brought my mule to the porch, and there, at the Captain's command, I carried the corpse out from the church and laid it across the animal's back.

"Now, sirrah," said the Captain, "if you want your mule again you will have to follow it to Valladolid."

So, once more, I paced that fateful road, and once more I passed through the trim portals of the Inquisition prison from which—as a nobleman—I had so recently escaped, and which I now reentered as a free but ignoble man—a poor *buhonero*, unworthy of consideration or courtesy, for, having delivered my burden and having assisted, as the jailer jokingly said, to place Don Fernando de la Mina into the coffin that he had so prettily decorated for himself that afternoon, I was dismissed by the callous varlets without thanks or reward.

Chapter 4
The Venta de la Reina

I was in the city of Valladolid, and it was now too late in the evenings for me to attempt to make my exit from the city through any of the gates. So I determined to seek a suitable shelter for the night in one of the *ventas,* the poorest kind of inn in the lower part of the town. Leaving the prison I again traversed the narrow street toward the river, and led my little mule into the stable-yard of the Venta de la Reina, a poor kind of inn where men of my class generally congregated. There, in the *cocina*—the dark little kitchen at the rear—I cooked the food that I had purchased, and then, settling down to my frugal meal, I began to sort out the contents of my *buhoneria*, and discovered that, beside the mule and her trappings, my sole worldly possessions now consisted of a goodly stock of saleable odds and ends, some cheap finery, and nine golden pieces of money. Five pieces that I had reserved from my own purse and four that I now discovered hidden between the wood and the lining of my poor dead predecessor's *buhoneria*.

These humble possessions, my son, formed the initial foundations of our present prosperous business, and I pray you to remember this whenever you are tempted to despair, and more particularly whenever you are tempted to "despise the day of small things." But all this is by the way, for by far the most serviceable of my new discoveries was a dirty little bundle of receipted bills made out to one "Timoteo Pereño." It was the possession of these bills that gave me the credentials of a new name and a new identity.

Don Fernando de la Mina was now dead to the world and to me. Henceforward, I was destined to assume the name and the humble personality of Timoteo Pereño—the traveling peddler—whoever he might be! So that evening, at the Venta de la Reina, I began to associate familiarly with my fellow *buhoneros*, and, as Timoteo, the traveling peddler, I now discreetly sought to learn from them the language and the manners of our craft.

I listened attentively to their simple tales of trade and travel, and I noted the peculiarities of their cajoling and piquant phraseology. Then, by dint of careful questionings and suggestions, I tactfully elicited from them some of the essential parts of my own past history as an itinerant peddler and thus I gradually began to know what type of man I really was and what was likely to be expected of me from my fellows. Thus I spent the first evening of my new life as a *buhonero*.

The Venta de la Reina was just an ordinary one—a mere roofed hovel opening out upon a stable-yard where my mule and a dozen others were stalled. There were no seats or tables and the "guests" just lay about upon the filthy floor with their saddles for pillows and their saddle bags as coverings.

So I lay there late into the night, talking with one and another, until, at last, exhausted with excitement and fatigue, I endeavored to forget the dirt, the noise, the stench, and the vermin, and then, commending myself and my loved ones to God's continued care, I fell into a peaceful and refreshing sleep.

Chapter 5
The Auto de Fé

When I woke up in the morning the sun was shining gloriously. It was Sunday morning—the morning of the Grand Auto de Fé—and, as I lay thinking awhile, I remembered that, but for the intervention of the Almighty God, I should have been one of the thirty victims condemned to be burned at the stake that day at the *Quemadero*. Burned alive in the presence of the King and his Court!

"The King!"—thought I—"the King!"

And then I recalled how graciously the Regent-Princess Joanna had received my obeisance to the King two years ago. The King! "Yes," I resolved, with a sudden inspiration, "Yes, I will, as a *buhonero*, attend the Auto de Fé. I will get there early and take my stand near the royal platform and, as soon as the King arrives, I will approach him, and I will reveal to him God's marvelous intervention and then openly confess myself to His Catholic Majesty. I will plead my father's valor and sacrifice for Spain. I will avow my loyalty to my King and Country and then throw myself upon the leniency and protection of His Majesty.

So, early on that Sunday morning, I took my place in the crowd of common people in the Great Square of Valladolid, just as the dismal bell began to toll its ominous signal. The soldiers were clearing a passageway for the priests and martyrs and, in the disturbance, I gradually elbowed my way right up to the royal platform just as the King arrived. His Majesty was followed by his sister, the Princess Joanna, his son the young Don Carlos, the foreign Ambassadors, and the ladies and gentlemen of the Court. Many of these had been my personal friends; some, indeed, had shared my recent birthday hospitality! But all of them—both friends and strangers—now knew unquestioningly that Don Fernando de la Mina, who had escaped from prison yesterday, had been caught and killed by the vengeance of God in the Church of Arroya de la Encomienda, and, in that belief and at the command of the Church, they had now come to witness the burning of his dead body as the Auto de Fé that day!

There was a hush and then a stir among the crowd as the procession marched into the plaza, led by the Dominicans carrying the crimson banner of the Inquisition. These were followed by sixteen "penitents," those who, at the last moment, had abjured their heresy. A somber company! Should I have been one of these? I dare not speculate; I can only thank God that He spared me the penitents' terrible trial of faith.

A great cross was now carried into the square and then appropriately following the cross, there came the twelve men and two women martyrs, who now advanced to the Tribune to receive their sentence of death. Some of these victims were scholarly folk of noble rank. The very flower of Spanish manhood and womanhood. But all of them were barefooted; they had rope round their necks and all but one were garbed in the *san-benito*—that hideous yellow smock with flames and devils painted on it. After this "noble army of martyrs" had marched past, there filed into the square twenty or thirty lay fanatics, who bore between them the seven black coffins that I had assisted to paint with the symbols of Hell in the prison courtyard yesterday; and in one of which it was now universally believed the Divinely stricken body of Don Fernando de la Mina lay.

I will not dwell upon the final horrors of that Sabbath-day drama. Let it suffice that, after the Bishop of Zamora had preached a sermon upon the true faith, sentence of confiscation of property and varied terms of imprisonment were pronounced upon the sixteen penitents, who were then conducted back to prison, some for years and some for life.

The staunch and unrepentant fourteen martyrs were next arraigned before the Inquisitors, and a final appeal was made to them to renounce their heretical faith. At this last dread moment the awful fear of suffering overcame the courage of twelve of those fourteen martyrs, and to these twelve was accorded the solace of the *garrote*; that is to say, they were permitted to be strangled before they were thrown to the flames.

Then the two Christian heroes advanced who had scorned to compromise with conscience and whose constancy had triumphed to the last. They were sentenced to be burned alive!

One of these was Father de Roxas, a Dominican monk, the son of the Marquis de Poza. He advanced proudly towards the royal and the official platforms, and, having received his sentence, he was stripped of his priestly robe and dressed in the *san-benito*. Then, standing there with head erect and outstretched hand, he began an oration in defense of the Reformed Doctrine. But before he had spoken more than a few words he was silenced, gagged, and removed to the *Quemadero* and burned alive!

Then the second Christian hero advanced. He was my old friend and first instructor in the Faith, a Florentine nobleman who had married my cousin and lived in Valladolid. A pure, kindly, brave Christian soul. His name rang out from the Tribunal: "Señor Don Carlos de Seso!" and he advanced quietly, proudly, firmly, until he came to the royal seat.

There he stood still for a moment and then, looking up to the King, he said, with a loud, clear voice: "Sire! Why do you consent to have your innocent subjects thus burned at the stake?"

The King looked scornfully upon him and replied in slow, measured words: "Yo trahere la leña para quemar á mi hijo, si fuere tan malo como usted."

My son, I heard the King reply to Don Carlos de Seso's rebuke in these very words: "I would bring the faggots to burn my own son, were he as wicked as you."

Procession at the Auto de Fé.

Do you wonder that my heart sank within me when I heard these unkingly words? I had come to the Auto de Fé on that Sabbath morning hoping to win the clemency of my sovereign. But now I knew, only too well, that I had no hope of pity or justice from the blind and heartless bigotry of my priest-ridden King.

Henceforth, my only assurance of safety was to be sought in an escape from Spain. I must escape from Catholic Spain swiftly and secretly and seek safety beyond the Pyrénées in Protestant Navarre; and there await the arrival of my beloved Doña Rosa de Riello and start my life anew in an alien land.

Chapter 6
The Plazuela del Hospicio

With a heavy heart I walked away toward the river—a forlorn and solitary outcast—and there I tried—but tried in vain—to formulate my plan of escape. Gradually I began to realize the awful truth that I was alone, an unknown stranger in the midst of kindred and friends—but with no hope of help or pity from a single living soul. I could not think clearly, I was too bewildered and depressed by the awful scenes that I had so recently witnessed; and now a deepening sense of my own utter loneliness increased my misery as I begun to realize my true position. I had become a new creature without a history and without a friend! Oh! How I longed for companionship and sympathy! If I had but one friend to whom I could confide my sorrow and my secret! And my heart burned with a feverish desire to acquaint my beloved with the fact of my marvelous deliverance and safety. My heart ached as I thought that, at that very moment, she was mourning my death and the loss of all the sweet happiness we had so fondly dreamed and hoped together.

As I thus meditated, two women drew near to where I was standing. They were dressed in black. One was deeply veiled, and I did not recognize her; but the maid, who was unveiled, I immediately recognized as Ana, the faithful old servant of my beloved. The two women walked a little way beyond me by the river and then they turned quickly into the Plazuela del Hospicio. There they joined the little group of passengers who had come in from the country that morning to witness the Auto de Fé, and who were now waiting to return home by the *galera*—the country wagon—that plies between Valladolid and Simancas. I followed my beloved and her maid into the square and stood beside them in the crowd, and as I looked upon the sorrowful face of the Doña Rosa and the weary, hopeless look upon Ana's countenance, I was sorely tempted to reveal myself to them and transform their sorrow into joy. But I dared not—the truth of my escape was so unbelievable! They would, perhaps, think me an impostor, or the perpetrator of cruel jest; and even should I be able to convince them that it was I, Don Fernando de la Mina, who confronted them, the shock and sudden happiness might overwhelm them and bring us to disaster. Alas! Now that I had the opportunity of revealing myself to my beloved—an opportunity for which I had so fervently prayed—I was unable to use it. In vain I strove to devise some means of arresting her attention, but my heart and my senses failed me.

The passengers were now moving toward the ladder that was being set up against the wagon and, as the passengers moved toward it, each engrossed with his or her own affairs, I drew near to the Doña Rosa and, raising my hat, said: "Señora, will you condescend to hear the simple words of a poor *buhonero*, a man who, though neither *Morisco* nor *Gitano*, possesses the mystic gift of seeing clearly into the future? Believe me, Señora, the darkness of your present hour is but the prelude of a brighter day."

As I spoke she looked tenderly but searchingly upon me, and I knew that she was remarking in my face a strange likeness to one whom she had devoutly loved and whom she now deemed dead to her. But her transient expression of sweet surprise soon faded into a settled look of sorrowful resignation as she replied: "Señor, I thank you for your kindly sympathy, but the light has gone out from my earthly life—the dead do not return!"

Then, opening her purse, she gave me a silver piece and bade me, "*Adios,* Señor, and may the blessing of God abide with you." And as I stood watching the *galera* pass out from the square, I strove hard to devise some means whereby I might continue my communication with her.

Chapter 7
The Temptation of Don Juan de Lario

For several moments after the departure of my beloved and her maid, I continued to stand listlessly in the Plazuela del Hospicio. At last I resolved to return to my squalid quarters at the Venta de la Reina. But just as I passed across the square two men entered it: Father Lorenzo, a distant priestly cousin of mine, and Don Juan de Lario.

The two men walked toward me side by side, one garbed in solemn black with a curled-brimmed hat and a flowing cassock; and the other ornately attired in a rose velvet doublet and cinnamon hose. The latter was Don Juan, my cousin, and he was also the cousin of Father Lorenzo. His estates joined my beloved's and mine at Simancas. He, too, like myself, had accepted the Reformed Faith under the guidance of Don Carlos de Seso (who had married his sister), and he and I had always been close friends and neighbors together.

The two men crossed the little square and entered the *vino*—the little wine shop—at the corner. Instinctively I followed them and, as they seated themselves near the entrance, I passed by them and went right into the further end of the shop.

Now it so happened that the wind set in toward me and from where they sat, and—although they spoke quietly—I was able to overhear every word of their conversation.

"No! No!" said the priest. "No, no, Juan. It is useless for you to appeal to, what you call, my 'natural affection.' The obligations of family relationship ceased for me the moment I became a son of the Holy Catholic Church. My vows, my earthly interests, and my hopes of Heaven safeguard me from such weakness and false pity. The secrets of the Holy Office, which I keep inviolate, and the authority of the Church, which I unswervingly obey, forbid me to say more than I have already told you, and I repeat that every traitor—note, *every traitor*—who communicates the poisonous heresy of that Anti-Christ Luther will be exterminated in the fires of the Inquisition. The Holy Church and the Secular Powers are irresistibly allied to that end. You heard what His Most Catholic Majesty said to the accursed Don Carlos de Seso, this morning—"

"No, I did not," replied Don Juan, "for I did not attend the Auto de Fé."

"That fact," replied the priest, "is well known to the Holy Office, and it is your absence from the Auto de Fé, and your past association with de Seso, that have brought you under suspicion of heresy. Yet," he continued, "yet, despite your defection, and your contemptuous neglect of this Most Holy Sacrament—for Sacrament it is—the Church graciously offers you a complete pardon if you will secretly inform the Holy Office of the heresy and the source of the Doña Rosa de Riello. And now, my dear Juan"—and here a gleam of wondrous kindness shone upon the priest's countenance as he reached across the table and tenderly touched the young man's arm—"*Acuérdate primo hermano mio*, let me urge you for the last time to confess and recant your past heresy; throw yourself upon the mercy of the Church and I will secure for you full absolution and readmission into the safety and the blessedness of the Holy Catholic Faith. Remember, my son, that if you refuse to obey the Church in this matter, you will imperil your present and your eternal welfare. You will be tortured and condemned, your body will be given to the flames and your property will be confiscated, your name shall go down to posterity in perpetual infamy, and your soul in Hell shall be denied the saving rites of the Christian Church. Now you must make up your mind speedily—indeed, you must decide on confession or contumacy before midnight tomorrow, for at midnight tomorrow you will be arraigned before the Holy Inquisition. I have warned you! Now do not be deceived, there is no chance of escape. You are watched night and day."

From the dark corner where I sat sipping my wine I watched Don Juan's face, and saw him wince, as well he might, under that terrible threat. But I did not despise him for his fear, or even for his seeming dalliance with a hideous temptation—a temptation to save his own life, his property and good name, at the price of a treachery that would destroy the life of my beloved and all our hopes of happiness in this world.

How patient that priest was! He waited and waited for a reply. But Don Juan continued to sit in silence for at least a quarter of an hour. Then, at last, the young man rose without a word, paid for the wine and went out into the Plazuela alone. Father Lorenzo watched him go, then he, too, arose and departed, leaving me perplexed and fearful for the safety of my beloved. What should I do? What could I do? One certainty fixed itself in my mind. My beloved would be informed against before midnight tomorrow.

If I attempted to write to her, my letter would be intercepted, for she, too, was being watched! Beside this, writing was now impossible for me. Never could a *buhonero* in Spain even write so much as his own name, and if I incautiously called for a pen and ink at the wine shop, or even at the Venta, suspicion would immediately fall upon me and I should be watched—for the common people at that time were only too glad of any opportunity to inform against a foe or a stranger, in order to ingratiate themselves with the powerful priests and secure as the reward of their treachery a fourth part of the condemned victim's confiscated property. Heresy, or even the semblance of heresy, was such a dangerous thing in those perilous times of excited fanaticism.

Chapter 8
Love Contends with Loyalty

B ut how could I communicate with the Doña Rosa? Every avenue of approach seemed closed to me. Bu the need was urgent. It was imperative that I should, at once, inform her of the danger that threatened her.

For some time I continued to sit in the wine shop pondering how I could let her know what I had just heard. As I sat and pondered, I happened to look unconsciously out through the open doorway of the *Vino* and into the sunlit square beyond, and there, in the further corner of the Plazuela, I noticed a crowd of peasants standing round an old man who sat at a table in the shade of one of the arches. He was the *escribano*, the professional writer and reader of letters—for you must know that the ignorant multitudes of Spain can neither read nor write, and must needs employ someone to do their correspondence.

Quickly I paid for my wine and went out toward the *escribano*, and waited there in the crowd until he was free to serve me. Then I directed him to write a letter for me to "The Señora Ana, maid to the Doña Rosa de Riello," and say: "Señora, the *buhonero* whom you honored by your kindness at Valladolid today desires to return to you a very valuable trinket that you lost as you entered the *galera* in the Plazuela del Hospicio. The *buhonero* will be at Simancas tomorrow at noon and will wait for you there with the trinket outside the Fonda de la Rosa."

I signed this missive with a cross, but underneath the cross I added my secret *cifra*—a flourished F.M. with which I had always concluded my letters to the Doña Rosa. This I did in the hope that Ana would surely show the unexpected message to her mistress. However, the messenger whom I dispatched with my letter returned in the evening with only this bald reply: "The mistress Ana said, "Tell the *buhonero* that I will meet him tomorrow at noon.""

So next morning I rode my mule to Simancas and there I found the faithful Ana waiting for me outside the Fonda de la Rosa. Inviting her into the quiet shade of the *puerta*, I inquired: "Did you show my letter to the Doña Rosa?"

"No," she replied, "I destroyed it immediately lest it should be seen by one of the servants. My mistress desires that her visit to Valladolid shall remain unknown to anyone but me." Then, turning abruptly to the matter in hand, she asked: "Have you brought the trinket?"

Guardedly I inquired: "Did you lose one?"

To this direct question she required with perfect frankness: "I do not know for certain, but I may have lost one, and, if you will describe the trinket you have found, I will claim it if it belongs to my mistress."

"Oh, no!" said I. "If it belongs to your mistress you must surely know what it is like. I will help you, if I may. Will you describe to me the jewels that, perhaps, you might have lost?"

And, without any hesitation, she began to enumerate first, several rings and ornaments (many of which had been my personal gifts to my beloved), and then proceeded to describe some of the valuable old heirlooms which I remembered to have seen so often at the Castillete de Riello.

This ingenuous admission showed me clearly that the Doña Rosa had already contemplated flight, and that she and Ana had visited Valladolid yesterday for the wise purpose of conveying her portable valuables away from Riello in order to deposit them in a secret place of safety somewhere in or near Valladolid.

I now had to admit that none of the jewels she enumerated was the one that I had discovered. This seemed to relieve Ana's mind and she, thereupon, prepared to bid me farewell. But I quietly detained her and, speaking very low said: "Señora, I am certain that the trinket in my keeping is a priceless and essential possession of the Doña Rosa de

Reillo. Yesterday, immediately after your departure from Valladolid, I discovered in the Plazuela del Hospicio a talisman that can serve and save her alone. Its possession will avert from her impending disaster and death."

Then I repeated to Ana the conversation that I had overheard yesterday between Father Lorenzo and Don Juan de Lorio in the wine shop, and I impressed upon her the necessity of the Doña Rosa's immediate escape from imminent arrest.

Ana, that good, noble, loyal old servant and friend, received my confidence with evident caution and betrayed no fear or great concern. She thanked me and bade me farewell, but would not reveal to me anything concerning my beloved's present circumstances or intentions.

Then she turned to depart, but, as she turned she gave a quick second glance at my anxious and unguarded face, and I felt conscious that she, like her mistress, was strangely impressed by my resemblance to one whom they knew to be dead. Again she looked searchingly at me, feeling safe to do so in her certain knowledge of Don Fernando's death. Then, with a sense of surprise and pleasure revealed upon her dear old homely face, she spoke with a kindlier, but still guarded, confidence, and said: "If you really desire to help my mistress it might, perhaps, be well if you keep yourself in touch with us. You seem to be honest and of gentle behavior—but you are poor! If you will faithfully serve my mistress she will reward you generously. To that end I should wish you to return with me to the Castillete de Riello in order that you may personally present your talisman to the Doña Rosa."

This trap was cleverly devised, my son! I know the subtle workings of the Spanish mind. Once inside the Castillete and, were I friend or foe, I should be absolutely in their power! But, oh! How my heart leaped at the prospect of again seeing my beloved and helping her to safety and happiness!

Chapter 9
The Castillete de Riello

With the difference due to Ana from a mere *buhonero*, I followed her at a respectful distance, walking with my mule along the Tordesillas road and then down the long avenue of chestnut trees that forms the private entrance to the old Castillete de Riello. How I strained my eyes to see my beloved in the gardens or at any of the windows! But no such happy vision blessed my expectations. Nor, when we reached the house, was there any sight or sound of her. I followed Ana through the familiar patio and into my lady's parlor, then into the servant's quarters, but the Doña Rosa was nowhere to be found.

The whole place seemed to be haunted, as though it were under some evil spell. Instead of the quiet, ordered industry common to the Castillete there was now fitful loud talking and confusion everywhere. The farm laborers and the servants of the household were crowded in the kitchen, some shouting, some speaking in frightened, agitated whispers, and as we entered they all shrank away from us in fear. But the moment they recognized Ana they came toward her and cried: "Oh, Mistress Ana, the officers of the Holy Inquisition are searching the house! Don Juan came here in haste at noon—he spoke hurriedly to our mistress, and since then we have not been able to find her anywhere."

"O! no!" thought I. "So my noble young cousin has scorned the priest's traitorous temptation to betray the Doña Rosa and instead, has bravely come to forewarn my beloved of her danger. The officers have arrived here and are searching for evidence that will assist their midnight examination of Don Juan and, perhaps, help them to wring from their victim admissions that will establish the heresy of the Doña Rosa!"

I looked round upon the laborers and the servants of the Riello household as they stood there in the hall.

Genuine love and fear were expressed on every countenance. The women wept and the men stood sullen and savage. Perceiving their loyalty I determined to utilize it. So, speaking first to one and then another, I gradually roused the latent courage of the men, and proposed that the eight of us should surprise and overpower the four officers of the Inquisition—bind them and secure them in one of the lofts, in order to give the Doña Rosa time to make her escape.

But, good Lord! Before I had finished stating my plans, the men, by dint of paltry breed and ignorance, began to hesitate. The little pluck and unselfishness that I had been able to stimulate within them quickly subsided before their superstitious fears, and presently, when the searchers of the Holy Office descended into the patio, the poor craven loons shrank away one by one into the recesses of the dimly lighted kitchen.

Oh how I cursed their cowardice! But, hoping still to rally them, I dragged the long heavy kitchen table to one side of the doorway, and the meal chest to the other, and then drew the curtain across the window so that when the officers should come into the room, single file, as they needs must, and then grope their way forward in the darkness, we should have them trapped and hampered in a narrow space, where we could surprise and overcome them by sheer weight and numbers. But, just as the officers approached the kitchen door, Ana gripped my arm and said: "Don't attempt resistance. It is hopeless—and quite unnecessary, for Doña Rosa has already escaped, and is now quite safe from arrest or detection."

Then she led away through the small service door into a narrow lane that skirts the older portion of the Castillete. Here she bade me assist her to mount my mule and run beside her into the high road until we reached the beginning of a rough cart-track that led to one of the Riello farms. There she hastily dismounted and bade me hold the mule and await her return.

As Ana departed in the deepening shade the grim humour of the situation gradually dawned on me, and I began to laugh merrily to myself as I thought how I, an erst-while nobleman of Spain, was now acting as a servile lackey to my lady's maid! And, with that strange revulsion of feeling that sometimes accompanies distress, I laughed again and again at this ludicrous perversion of fortune until at last, the return of sober sense compelled me once more to recognize the stern reality that poverty, ignominy, rags, and degradation had now come into my life as final and irrevocable facts.

Chapter 10

Don Juan's Arrest

I think I must have sat there by the roadside nearly an hour when I heard faint sounds from the direction of the Castillete de Riello—sounds that warned me that horsemen were approaching. So, withdrawing quietly into the shadow of the stone wall, I drew my mule toward me and gently caressed her ears to keep her motionless. Presently, in the pale moonlight, I saw the Captain of the Inquisition Guard and three of his men approach and then ride past me escorting my unhappy cousin to his midnight interview with the Inquisitors at Valladolid!

Gradually the sound of the grim cavalcade died away in the silence, and darkness soon enveloped the little company. Then, as I sat in the quiet of my lonely vigil, I fell to meditating upon the probable fate of Don Juan de Lario. Would he betray my beloved or would he play the man? Would he deem it consistent with his honour that, having already forewarned the Doña Rosa of her impending danger, he might seek his own safety by divulging the facts he knew concerning her heresy? Did he betray her that night or did he play the man? I have often wondered, and now, after forty years, I wonder still; for I have never been able to discover his fate! The Holy Office works so silently and secretly!

While I was thus meditating upon my cousin's forthcoming ordeal, my reverie was disturbed by two women who approached me from the farm. Had I not expected them I should never have recognized my beloved and her maid in the two sturdy, rural beldames who now confronted me. They were both of them dressed in long black hooded traveling cloaks, such as peasant women wear—their feet were shod with clumsy country boots and each of the women was carrying a huge bundle of luggage. Had I not expected them I should certainly have allowed them to pass by me unrecognized. However, without pretense at not knowing them, I immediately advanced toward the dames and courteously knelt to kiss the Doña Rosa's hand, then I quickly told her of Don Juan's arrest, and at her request I repeated the conversation that I had overheard yesterday between Father Lorenzo and Don Juan de Lario.

The Doña Rosa listened to me without surprise or comment, and then bade me quickly pack my mule with the bundles that she and Ana had brought with them, saying: "I wish you to convey these packages to the Fonda de la Natividad at Valladolid. You will wait for us there in the courtyard and I will then reward you for your courtesy and your service."

How strangely imperious her command sounded to my unaccustomed ear! At first I felt inclined to resent her preemptory treatment, but, on second thoughts, I recognized that I really had no right to any gentler treatment than is usually accorded to a casual laborer of the meanest rank and such, in truth, I had now become... Nonetheless, so irritating and distasteful to me was the new distinction that had arisen between us, that just for one moment I stood and hesitated to obey. But the Doña Rosa did not deign to notice my hesitancy; with quiet dignity she calmly moved away and left me to gather up her bundles and pack my little mule.

Obediently to her command I now proceeded slowly along the road, keeping only just a little in advance of the women, so as to be able to afford them protection if it should prove necessary. As I drew near to the city gate, however, I hastened on alone, for I knew that, as Timoteo Pereño the *buhonero*, I could, by bestowing the usual flagon of wine and a few coins in the corner of the guard-room, pass through the gate unchallenged with my bundles.

Having thus safely entered the city I hurried along to the Fonda and waited for the women in the courtyard of the inn. While I was standing there beside my little mule, the ostler of the Fonda sidled toward me. He was an obsequious, crafty, simple-looking loon, and he sauntered up to me, with an air of easy unconcern, and asked about my business and the business of the two women who were employing me.

"Oh," said I, "they are just a couple of farmer's wives. Don't you know them?"

To which he replied, with a sinister smile, "I only know that they came here yesterday and engaged a bedroom. Have you worked for them before?"

"Yes," said I "but"—and then happily this conversation was suddenly interrupted by a loud peal of the bell, announcing the arrival of the dames in question. The ostler, without moving, made the usual demand: "*Quien es?* Who's there?" and through the wicket-grille Ana's voice spoke the, then correct, response "*Dos Cristianas.*" Thereupon the ostler pulled the cord that hung beside him in the patio and released the wicket-latch and so admitted my beloved and her maid.

The women came to where I stood waiting with my mule, but the ostler still remained close to us, listening to our talk and generally evincing a curiosity that bade us no good. However, he learned very little, for Ana immediately unloaded the mule, and then, handing the heavier bundles to me, she bade me follow her up the patio stairway and along the open gallery that surrounded the patio and into the room that they had engaged the day before. It was just an ordinary brick-floored sleeping room and contained a couple of alcove beds, a table, some stools and a large clothes chest, in which I now had no doubt, were safely secreted the valuable heirlooms and jewelry from the Castillete de Riello, which my beloved and Ana had evidently brought with them from Simancas on the previous day.

Chapter 11
The Silver Key

When I had completed my service to the Doña Rosa she generously rewarded me with a gold piece—a guerdon far beyond the value of my work. Then she bade me a *decisive* farewell. There was no mistaking it! Her demeanor and the studied emphasis of her words told me all too plainly that she intended this to be my final service to her. Before leaving her, however, I expressed a desire that she would again honour me with her confidence and commands. But to this appeal she merely replied: "My future movements are very uncertain."

And beyond that statement I could get no further satisfaction.

I was now sadly perplexed and baffled in my efforts to keep in touch with her. She had become suspicious of the willing and zealous *buhonero*, and she evidently feared that I already knew too much concerning her, and she had, therefore, prudently (as she thought) determined to quickly separate herself and Ana from me by a sudden, unexpected departure from Valladolid.

So, in my distress and emergency, I descended into the patio of the Fonda and there sought the assistance of the surly ostler. Confiding in him as one fellow servant to another I said:

"*Hermano mio*, my brother, will you do me a friendly turn? Those two women owe me a considerable sum of money for carrying, and I have good reason to believe that they intend to escape from here without paying me. My name is Timoteo Pereño and I am loading at the Venta de la Reina near the river. If you will come and inform me the moment you know of their intention to depart, I will give you a couple of *reales* for your trouble," and thereupon shook hands with the scoundrel and departed with my mule to the Venta de la Reina.

Verily, my son, it is truly said in the land of my birth, "A silvery key opens every door in Spain!"—as you will presently see.

During the early part of that night I suffered great anxiety in my mind. I could not banish the brooding thought that if my beloved should manage to escape me now we should never meet on earth again. She would certainly be captured by the officers of the Inquisition, for it was quite impossible that she and Ana could travel undiscovered along the three hundred miles of country that now lay between them and safety. Every town guard en route would be forewarned of their intention to pass through the city gates and even the remote villages upon the side roads would be made acquainted with the fact that the Doña Rosa de Riello, a wealthy heretic, and her maid, were attempting to escape from Spain into Protestant Navarre.

Escape from Spain in those dreadful days of religious persecution was always difficult. Even for an experienced traveler it was always perilous and fraught with momentary danger; and it would be quite impossible for two frail women who had never before ventured more than twenty miles away from their home. Even for a man like myself, who was now comparatively safe from pursuit by the known fact of my death, even for me I knew that capture and death awaited me on my first false or suspicious move anywhere south of the Pyrénées. As for the women, it was all too evident to me that their present method of disguise and procedure were foredoomed to speedy failure. They were so commonplace and so obvious to the simplest adversary. A "frontal attack" upon any of the great city gates, even under the cleverest disguise, would sooner or later bring about their detection and arrest.

The difficulties of our flight were multiplied by the fact that there were now three of us to escape and that, unfortunately, we three were not under the same direction. The difficulty of effecting a triple escape in such circumstances was tremendous and the prospect far from propitious. However, it is always well to remember that in all life's difficulties both success and failure lie equally implicit in every human emergency, and just as we wisely or unwisely cope with an emergency, so do we win from it either success or failure.

Now it was perfectly certain to me that our only possible way of escape from peril was by the slow and cautious method. By the patient creating of a local confidence and then the quick taking of whatever opportunities might occur. Vigilance, patience, daring, quickness, calmness, and the power or dissimulation, were the essential elements of a successful escape—and these qualities my beloved did not possess!

No, I must keep near her and protect and guide her. Beginning as a stranger, I must gradually win her confidence and then personally direct her way into safety, and then, and not till then, must I venture to reveal myself to her.

"But if" thought I, with a sudden start of fear, as I lay ready for sleep on the filthy straw that lay scattered over the Venta floor—"But if...if?"—and here, drawing my tattered cloak more closely round me, I repressed my futile and distressful thoughts, and then prayerfully seeking wisdom, and reposing my hope in God's continued mercy, I fell into a peaceful sleep.

Chapter 12
On the Road to Cabezón

Early next morning I was sitting in the brilliant sunshine at the doorway of the Venta making my frugal meal of bread and onion, when I saw the ostler of the Fonda de la Natividad come hurrying to inform that the women "had already departed from the inn."

"They had," he said, "ridden away upon a couple of mules that they had hired from him"—and here the cunning scoundrel became silent until I had given him the promised bribe! Then, continuing his information, he told me that the women had ordered him to fetch back his mules that night from Cabezón, a little town about ten miles north of Valladolid. You will see it marked on the map that I have roughly sketched here for your better understanding of the route I followed in my escape from Spain.

Within two minutes of receiving this vital information I was astride my little mule and hastening northward along the great Burgos road; but ride as hard as I could it was not until nearly midday that I first caught sight of the women. They were toiling ahead of me along the dusty sun-blazed road about a mile this side of Cabezón, and they were just preparing to rest awhile under the trees at the foot of the hill that rises toward the town.

Following their good example, I too, reined in my mule and dismounted in a wayside cattle hovel, which conveniently screened me from their observation and, at the same time, afforded me an uninterrupted view of the main road in both directions. The women's siesta in the cool shade was of very brief duration, however, for they soon arose to proceed on their journey. As soon as they were on the move I, too, prepared to mount my mule—but just as I was starting to follow them I noticed a small cloud of dust rising on the road behind me, about a quarter of a mile away in the direction of Valladolid, whence we had just come. Presently I heard the hasty clip-clop of a horse's hoofs, and in a few moments I saw a sturdy horseman flash past the hovel. He was the Captain of the Inquisition Guard!

Yesterday the Doña Rosa had cleverly outwitted him. But now, thanks to the treachery of the surly ostler (one of the myriad low spies in the pay of the Holy Office and the one who alone could know my lady's intended destination); thanks to that recent treachery the Captain of the Inquisition Guard now had my beloved completely at his mercy. He was already drawing rein near the women, and would certainly arrest my beloved unless I, an unarmed *buhonero*, could instantly devise some means to outmaneuver him.

Quickly grasping the possibilities of the situation, I at once urged my little mule to her utmost pace, and came to within twenty feet of the Captain. He looked round at me, and, seeing only a *buhonero*, he took no further heed. Then he dismounted from his horse—for courtesy compelled him to dismount in the presence of my beloved, who was now standing in the road—he then removed his hat with one hand and with the other presented his official warrant to the Doña Rosa, saying, as he stood with both his hands extended before him: "Señora Doña Rosa de Riello, it is with sincere regret that I must request you to return with me to Valladolid. If you will read this warrant that I have the honour to show you, you will, I am sure, submit to its authority without demur."

My beloved stood before the Captain as one petrified with horror. There seemed no hope of escape.

The Captain, a tall, powerful man, was armed with a couple of pistols, but happily he had not deemed it necessary to handle them for the arrest of two unarmed women, and so the pistols remained in their cases at either side of his saddle.

The Captain, as I have already said, was a tall and very powerful man, while I, on the other hand, was but a slightly built and unarmed man.

There stood the sturdy Captain, his broad back turned toward me and his hands outstretched before him! To me it was a tempting attitude—an attitude that suddenly prompted a happy flash of memory recalling an old schoolboy trick that I, a wiry, delicate lad, had often played upon my bigger and stronger opponents in our rough-and-tumble play.

Quietly slipping from my saddle and approaching the Captain very stealthily from behind, I drew nearer and nearer to him. Then I suddenly sprang upon his back and flung my legs round his waist and gripped him tighter and tighter. In vain he struggled to throw me off. He tore at my legs with his finger and did me terrible damage but, in return, I squeezed his throat in a deadly grip until the combined pressure of my legs and my suffocating grip made the strong man stagger.

He now cleverly pretended to be on the point of collapse and made a lurch as if he were about to fall forward. But I knew by his skilful defense so far that he was far too well versed in such sport as this to accept defeat so easily. So I continued to keep a steady hold upon him until he was very nearly exhausted. Then he made a second feint of falling forward, but, instantly reversing it, by a sudden jerk backward he endeavored to fling himself upon the ground and crush me under the impact of his weight.

But, happily, I was forewarned of this move by early experience of the game, and, being very light in weight and as nimble as a cat, I sprang from his back while he was falling, and the very moment his body touched the ground I was instantly on top of him with the point of my knee pressing hard into the pit of his stomach. With one hand I again gripped his throat and with the other I seized his hair and then—lifting his uncovered head, I dashed it again and again upon the stones until he became unconscious.

Chapter 13
I Enter My Lady's Service

What strange folk women are! During the few minutes of my furious encounter with the sturdy Captain, the Doña Rosa and her maid stood stolidly looking on—just as if the fight has been an entertainment instead of the grim life-and-death struggle that it really was! And it was not until I had tied the Captain's hands and feet, and had confiscated his warrant and his pistols and had gagged him to ensure his silence, it was not until then that the women evinced any personal concern in the affair! Rising, hot and infuriated from the struggle, I approached Ana and asked her to help me, lift and drag the Captain from the roadway. Between us we pulled the unconscious Captain from the road and deposited him under the trees near the farm, where we were sure he would be found and secured before nightfall. I knew that I ran a tremendous risk in thus leaving the life in his body, and I was sorely tempted to put him to death. Had I yielded to that temptation we should have been spared much anxiety and our escape from Spain would have been comparatively easy. But if I had killed him, even in self-defense, I should have had an everlasting burden on my conscience. For, after all, the Captain was only discharging his duty as he understood it, and, even though he was a slave to bigotry and our inveterate foe, he was nonetheless a courteous and an honourable gentleman.

No, I have never taken human life, thank God, and though the Captain dogged our footsteps for several weeks afterwards, I have never regretted that when he was completely in my power I permitted him to live.

The Doña Rosa now drew near to me and I at once knelt to do her homage.

"Señor," said she, "I owe my present safety to the chivalry of one who is unknown to me. I do not remember that I ever showed you kindness. Why, then, have you risked your life and liberty for me?"

"Señora," I replied in vague, but perfect truthfulness, "last Saturday I was, myself, in imminent peril of death in the Church of Arroya de la Encomienda, and there, unknown to anyone but to him and me, Don Fernando de la Mina, by a great self-sacrifice, preserved for me my life and liberty. Do you wonder, Señora, that I was grateful to Don Fernando, and that I there and then swore that I would henceforth place my life and service at his command? Don Fernando accepted my vow, and there upon he directed me to go at once and seek the Doña Rosa de Riello, and place my life and duty at her command. And, now, in compliance with Don Fernando's last request I crave your Excellency's acceptance of my humble service."

I remained kneeling in the roadway as I spoke and the Doña Rosa, after listening earnestly to my appeal, now extended her hand toward me in token of her acceptance of my service and there, as I knelt in the roadway—there from my heart—I pledged my life and duty to my mistress just as joyfully as, three years ago, I had pledged my eternal love to her. Then I kissed her hand and rose from the dusty road a new and happier man.

But, as I rose, I perceived that my beloved was looking intently into my face—her countenance betoken a surprised and almost superstitious fear—and I knew that she had again detected in my unguarded countenance that strange likeness to Don Fernando de la Mina, a likeness that, despite my shaggy beard and poor attire, I could not completely efface. But her transient look of surprise soon faded away, as the absolute certainty of my death recurred to her mind and now, once more, the returning sad look of the lonely woman was all too eloquent of her sorrowful thought, "the light has gone out from my earthly life—the dead do not return!" Oh! How my heart yearned to reveal the wondrous truth to my beloved—but for her own dear sake I dared not.

But now, quickly, regaining her self-possession and realizing the need of instant flight, Doña Rosa at once proceeded to explain her plans to me. She had, she said, already provided herself and Ana with French costumes, and, now that I was to join the company, she explained that it would be necessary that I also should be appropriately disguised. She directed me therefore, first to have my beard pointed—an operation that Ana at once performed upon me in the roadway, much to our amusement. Then my mistress informed me that I must go into Cabezón and there leave at the Fonda the two mules that she had hired at Valladolid and, after that I must purchase suitable clothing for myself, while she and Ana would ride the Captain's horse northward along the Burgos road and change their dresses en route. Then, as a French lady and her maid traveling home to Paris, they would wait for me, their courier-servant, to overtake them early next morning at the Fonda de Nuestra Señora del Rosario, where they intended to lodge at the little town of Dueñasaeros, about twelve miles to the north of Cabezón.

As soon as they had departed I began to pack my little mule with their luggage and then I proceeded with it to Cabezón. As soon as I arrived in the town I went to the Fonda and there delivered the two hired mules. Then, from a Jew in the plaza, I purchased a faded but very serviceable doublet and hose, a soft hat, a pair of shoes, a long cloak and a rapier—all of which I rolled up into a rough bundle. Then, as a *buhonero*, I led my mule out from Cabezón and back again in the direction of Valladolid, as if it were my intention to return to the city.

My return journey soon brought me back to the scene of my recent fight with the Captain. There among the trees I changed my clothes and hid my rags and peddler's tackle in the undergrowth. Then, dressed as a respectable courier and leading my little mule, heavily laden with my lady's luggage, I prepared to retrace my steps in the wake of my French mistress and her maid.

Chapter 14

A Fool's Errand for the Captain

For some fell reason, however, I hesitated to depart from the scene of my recent encounter with the Captain. A strange fascination compelled me to linger there and—as it were—to react in fancy the desperate struggle I had had with my powerful foe. A curious restraint was upon me, and, as is unusual in such circumstances, either curiosity or the impulse of my conscience compelled me once more to seek my victim and ascertain how he was faring.

I knew that it was a foolish and a risky think to do, but the urge upon me was irresistible, and so I cautiously penetrated into the copse from tree to tree until I reached the spot where Ana and I and left the unconscious Captain.

Yes! There he lay, his massive body moving over from side to side. Evidently he had recovered consciousness and was now striving to wriggle his wrists free from the handkerchief with which I had tied them together behind his back. The scene fascinated me and, forgetting all else, I stood there for several moments watching his efforts, when, suddenly, to my intense dismay, he succeeded in freeing his hands. He rose to his feet, tore the gag and bandage from his mouth, and then, lurching forward to prevent himself from falling, he turned right round and looked me squarely in the face!

Instantly I raised my hat, saying that I had heard a strange noise and had just come into the copse from the roadway to investigate the cause. Was he injured? I inquired. Had thieves molested him? Could I render him any assistance?

He replied that he was the Captain of the Inquisition Guard and had been badly treated by enemies of the law and he desired me to release his ankles from the stout piece of harness rope with which I had securely bound him a couple of hours before. This done, he asked me if I had seen a stray horse wandering upon the road, and had I seen a couple of countrywomen with two laden mules?

I replied that I was a journeyman silversmith employed at Valladolid and had come from the city that afternoon in order to spend a short holiday with my parents who resided at Cabezón. No, indeed, I had not seen a stray horse on the road, but now that I came to think of it, I remembered that about an hour ago I passed two countrywomen about five miles or so from Valladolid. They were riding their mules towards the city and had a great deal of luggage strapped upon a large chestnut horse which they were drawing after them by the rein. "They seemed to be a curious cavalcade," I said, "and I wondered wherever they could be going to in such an unusual fashion. And further..."

But the Captain would not allow me to delay him "further." He hastily thanked me for my valuable information, for which he promised to reward me, and then set off at a good round pace, walking toward Valladolid.

I stood in the fading light and watched his burly form safely disappear into the darkness. Then, mounting my mule, I returned to Cabezón and passed unnoticed through the town and then proceeded northward through the night to Dueñasaeros, where, at the first glint of dawn, I was ringing the bell at the Fonda de la Nuestra Señora del Rosario, and inquiring for a French lady and her maid just as the Doña Rosa and Ana were descending into the patio to wait for me.

Quickly I told my mistress of the fool's errand upon which I had sent the Captain of the Inquisition Guard. My narrative amused her immensely and I was delighted to perceive that my astuteness had won from her an increased trust and appreciation of my devotion. Bidding me now seek refreshment and rest, she sent me to the servants' quarters at the Fonda and commanded me to attend her again in the patio at three o'clock.

When I rejoined her that afternoon she welcomed me kindly and then explained that, in order to acquit myself as a courier, I must learn to speak in the French tongue. "And," continued my beloved, with a winsome air of profound erudition, "as it will be necessary for you to learn to speak French as quickly as possible, I shall now begin to instruct you in that language."

Her naïve and presumptuous announcement was a choice piece of unconscious humour on the part of my beloved, for it was I who had taught her all the French she knew!

So with sweet ingenuousness my French mistress now seated herself complacently upon the padded leather settle in the patio corner and bade her willing pupil be seated on the little stool at her feet. Then, with a patronizing air of profound wisdom, she began to recite to me a few simple words and phrases in French and very, very slowly emphasized their correct pronunciation. "*Ecoutez*," said my lady, "*Oui Monsieur, Bonjour Madame, Dépêchez vous*," etc., etc., etc.

Appearing to marvel at my mistress's linguistic powers, and secretly tingling with suppressed merriment, I repeated the phrases one by one and mastered them all with a phenomenal rapidity and precision that would have aroused the suspicions of even the most accomplished teacher.

But the Doña Rosa—bless her sweet simplicity—the Doña Rosa was delighted with her success—and so was I!

And thus for several hours, on four successive days, she and I mutually enjoyed those delightful periods of intercourse and conversation.

I did not learn much French, it is true, but my artless teacher unconsciously allowed me to acquire some very much more desirable knowledge—knowledge, too, that was far more precious to me, for, as the lessons proceeded from day to day, I learned with deepening joy that a gracious sympathy was ripening apace between the teacher and her pupil. I could not fail to notice that the Doña Rosa found an ever-increasing pleasure in my company, as I gradually discarded the ignorance and awkwardness of a peasant and assumed once more the scholarship and easy behavior of a gentleman.

Chapter 15

Danger at Dueñasaeros

But the fourth evening of our pleasant stay at the little town of Dueñasaeros was a very critical period in our adventures.

During that day a stranger joined me in the servants' room. He was a fat and rather reticent fellow and proclaimed himself to be a lay-brother of the Convento de Miraflores at Burgos and servant of a priest who, he said, was due to arrive at the Fonda that evening. And sure enough about seven o'clock the gate bell rang. The lay-brother there upon rose slowly from his seat beside me and went out from our room into the patio in order to receive his superior. As he passed out I looked through the half-open doorway and perceived that the priest who was arriving at the Fonda was none other than Father Lorenzo! He whom I had overheard speaking with my cousin, Don Juan de Lario, in the wine shop at Valladolid a week before!

Instantly I suspected the purpose of his visit. The Captain of the Inquisition Guard, on his return to Valldolid four days before, had, of course, soon discovered the deception I played upon him on the evening of our fight, and now, having failed to trace the two countrywomen at either Valladolid or Cabezón, he and the priest were pushing their inquiries further northward to Dueñasaeros. The priest would seek for clues among the traveling guests at the various Fondas en route (the lay-brother learning all he could among the servants), while the Captain would search the roads and hold himself in readiness to effect our arrest at any moment.

Now, you must know that the servants' room at the Fonda (as is usual at Spanish inns) was set in from the patio just at the further end of the courtyard. It was a small and rather dark room and was lighted by a window that overlooked the corner of the patio and through this window we servants could see the table where the supper was now being laid, and, by listening very carefully, as servants generally do, we could hear most of the conversation of our masters in the patio. My lady, I could see, was already seated at table and the priest was now descending down the open stairway from his bedroom.

Presently, through the window, I overheard Father Lorenzo say, in our beautiful Castellano, "*Buenas noches, Señora*," to which my beloved aptly replied, in the French tongue, "*Bon soir, Monseigneur.*"

Then said the priest, accommodating himself to my lady's assumed tongue and speaking in most execrable French: "I hear, Madame, that you are returning to your home in Paris! I have a great many clerical friends there, and I should like to inquire who is your Father Confessor in Paris?"

"Father Ambrose, of St. Denis," replied the Doña Rosa with wonderful readiness.

"And to whom," persisted the priest, "to whom did he entrust your spiritual welfare at Valladolid eh? Do you remember?"

"No," replied Madame, who was evidently beginning to be disconcerted by the cunning priest's persistency, "I do not remember at the moment, Father, but I daresay I can tell you when I refer to my tablets after supper. But why do you ask?"

Why did he ask indeed! The reason was all too obvious—at least it was obvious enough to me! So without, staying to hear anymore, I hurried up to Ana's room, and, after telling all I had heard I bade her pack the luggage and valuables and these I at once carried down to the stables. Then I returned to Ana's room once more and bade her tell our mistress to plead indisposition and retire to her room immediately after supper.

Down in the stable the genial ostler now helped me to load my mule and, when he had pocketed the silver piece that I had given him for his trouble, we began chatting together familiarly and confidentially as fellow servants should. Said he, pointing across the patio to Father Lorenzo, who sat writing a letter at the further end of the supper table: "Some of these priests seem to think that servants like us ought to never to be tired! It is past eight o'clock and, would you believe it, just before you came into the stable the Father came and bade me get ready to ride to Valladolid and deliver a letter to the Captain of the Inquisition Guard. Twenty miles! Why, I shan't be there till midnight!"

"No," thought I, "you won't. But if you deliver your letter at midnight, the Captain will be here with his warrant by the morning."

So I quickly saddled the Captain's horse, and then went up to the women's room and told them to put on their cloaks and leave a light burning in their room, and then go and hide themselves in the bedroom, which was fortunately just at the top of the stairs. As soon as the women were safely hidden in my bedroom, I descended very slowly and solemnly into the patio and there, gravely approaching the priest, I said: "Father, the French lady to whom you spoke at supper-time is lying in her bedroom very seriously ill, and she desires to see you."

Now, Father Lorenzo, like every earnest priest, Roman or Protestant, was true to his sacred trust, and, cruel bigot though he was, he was ever ready to sacrifice himself in the cause of charity or suffering. As I approached him he turned his head and scrutinized me sternly. But when he saw my distressed look and heard my anxious appeal, he listened to my request with patience and sympathy. He immediately laid down his pen, then he pounced his unfinished letter with sand, folded it in his wallet, and prepared to follow me up the staircase intent only on ministering priestly solace to a suffering soul—and I almost hated myself for deceiving so sincere and kindly a man! But three innocent lives were at stake.

Respectfully I preceded him up the stairs and along the gallery and there I very, very slowly opened the door of Madame's empty room. Father Lorenzo, who was taken quite off his guard stepped unsuspectingly into the dimly lighted chamber—and I followed him! But just as I came near to the niche in the wall where the lighted bronze lamp stood, I carefully stumbled over something in the darkness and overthrew the lighted lamp upon the brick floor.

Profoundly humble in my whispered excuses, I begged that the Father would not venture to move in the darkness until I had brought another lighted lamp up from the kitchen. Then, groping my way to the door, I passed out and quietly secured it after me. Then I walked quickly along the gallery to my own bedroom and there, hastily gathering the women, I fled with them down the stairs and across the deserted patio into the stable. There, with the assistance of the ostler and me, the Doña Rosa and her maid mounted the Captain's large chestnut horse, while I bestrode my patient little mule.

We then bade a hasty *Adios* to the friendly ostler and hurried out through the back stable exit, before the priest could realize my purpose or raise an alarm to prevent our escape.

Had I delayed my maneuver even a couple of minutes the priest would have finished his letter and dispatched it by the ostler and then, in his absence, it would have been impossible for us to leave the Fonda that night, and we should assuredly have been arrested when the Captain arrived with his warrant in the morning!

Chapter 16
Suspicion among Friends

It was now nearly nine o'clock and a calm, cold night as we rode from the back exit of the warm stable into the Calle Vera Crux, and thence out upon the great north road that links Valladolid with Burgos. There on the open road beneath the starlit purple sky we three fugitives pressed on in silence hour after hour. Right through the night we rode, until a thin green thread of light on the eastern horizon heralded the dawn of day and warned us to leave the highway and pass into the less-frequented country road.

Cheered by the rising sun and gradually feeling more and more secure from immediate pursuit, we now began to talk about our recent perilous experience. But it was only Ana and I who talked and not the Doña Rosa. My lady remained strangely silent for quite a long time. She had evidently been thinking rather critically during the night, and now she suddenly turned to me and asked, with an air of marked suspicion: "Señor, how was it that you an uneducated *buhonero*, so readily understood the questions that you overheard Father Lorenzo ask me at supper time? He spoke in French, and he spoke very rapidly too! You could not have become sufficiently proficient in the language to understand it so well with only four days of tuition!"

This question was an embarrassing one and caused me to think awhile before I could answer it discreetly. Then, turning to her with an engaging smile I replied: "Señora, when I had the honour of addressing you in the Plazuela del Hospicio a few days ago, I was, in very truth a *buhonero* and nothing better than a *buhonero*—with only my rags and a peddler's pack as my sole possessions in the whole wide world. But, Señora, I should like you to know that before I fell to that low estate I had enjoyed a modicum of wealth and learning and had mixed with men and women in exalted stations of life. But, during the past few months I have suffered the severest and strangest vicissitudes of fortune. May it please you to know that six months ago, before disaster overtook me, I was a Spanish nobleman's confidential secretary! I held all his secrets and knew his innermost thoughts. He and I were identical in our aims and dispositions. It was I who wrote all his correspondence. Sometimes I wrote in Latin to his Lutheran friends in Germany, and sometimes in French to his brother at the Court of the Prince of Condé in Paris."

"Secretary!" interrupted Ana, "then why did you employ the public *escribano* to write that note you sent to me—and why, if you can write, why did you sign that letter with a cross?"

"Señora," I replied, addressing myself to the Doña Rosa, "Señora, I have learned discretion in a very hard school. Six months ago the nobleman whom I served was destroyed by the religious vengeance that now threatens you, and the same catastrophe that ruined him has also ruined and degraded me even to the condition of the poor *buhonero* whom you honoured by receiving into your service. Señora, in grateful fulfillment of Don Fernando de la Mina's behest, of which I have already told you, I have pledged my life and all that I have to the service of the Doña Rosa de Riello, and I hope to prove myself worthy of her confidence and to win advancement in my mistress's esteem equally with your Excellency's advancing fortunes."

The Doña Rosa listened to my proud speech with evident surprise, and with some slight show of indignation too, and she was just on the point of asking further awkward questions when our conversation was happily interrupted by the approach of a couple of countrywomen who passed across the road immediately in front of us. These women were laughing and singing and were followed by a group of talkative men and boys. They were, all of them, just about to start their day's work at the large olive farm which we ourselves were now approaching.

A man in the field, nearby, was leading an ox into the crushing shed. He opened the high barnlike doors and drove the ox through them, and then yoked the beast to the millbar and started him off upon his daily tramp round and round the crushing vat. Presently, some women entered the shed and proceeded to refill the vat with a fresh supply of olives and to adjust the panshons that received the oil which was now beginning to flow into them from the vents in the vat. And there everywhere around us the daily work of the farm began. Far away in the gardens on the rising ground men, women, and children were beating the trees with long rods. Some were up in the trees shaking the branches and some were picking up and basketing the olives that fell to the ground, while others were carrying heavy loads of the fruit toward the crushing mill.

Chapter 17
Pedro Detriño

We sat down by the roadside to watch this busy scene while we ate our morning meal. Presently I called one of the workers toward us and asked her to tell me the farmer's name.

"Señor Detriño, if it please your Excellency," said the woman.

"Well, that is fortunate," I replied, "for we have traveled all the way from Burgos during the night in order to transact business with Señor Detriño. Will you please conduct us to the *casa*?"

The woman laid her empty basket down and led the way through a couple of fields and then directed us to a rough track-road that led to Señor Detriño's home.

The farmer's house—like its owner—was small, solid and comfortable, and with a pervading air of success and generosity. At Detriño's invitation we all entered his business room and there I introduced myself to him as Pablo Acedo, an oil merchant trading at Tolosa. Then, half in jest, and wholly in anticipation, I looked affectionately into the face of my beloved and fondly informed the genial farmer that the Doña Rosa was my wife—the Señora Pablo Acedo—and Ana was her maid!

Quietly enjoying my beloved's suppressed embarrassment and quite heedless of the telltale dimple that always fell into my cheeks upon the slightest provocation, I proceeded to inform the oil-grower that, having heard his name mentioned in the Burgos market yesterday, I had journeyed hither in order to acquaint myself with the quality of his productions. Then I told him that if he would be willing to supply me with one jar each of the three qualities of his oil, I would purchase them and make him a cash payment at once provided he would help me to transport the three *tinajas*—three big earthenware jars—of oil to Burgos that day.

"Certainly," he replied. "Fortunately, I am well able to meet your requirements for it so happens that I am sending three jars of my second crushing to Burgos this evening, and I will send yours at the same time."

So I paid Detriño for the oil and in exchange I received from him a useful—a very useful—trade receipt—a trade receipt made out to "Señor Pablo Acedo" and signed in a good legible hand by "Pedro Clemente Detriño, y Sanata, y Meria" a pretentious signature that was really nothing but a grandiloquent string of old family names that betokened nothing of aristocracy but only a great deal of pride! How often such silly vanity as this betrays itself in men whose only claim to distinction lies in their commercial success! However, be that as it may, it was that receipt with "Detriño," etc.'s well-known signature upon it that was destined to serve my beloved and Ana and me as a letter of safe conduct into and out from the ancient, well-guarded city of Burgos.

Before we bade *Adios* to Detriño, I arranged with him that his men should meet us with the oil that evening at the place where the side road from his farm joins the main road to Burgos. Then, having thus far successfully concluded our business, we bade the genial oil-grower *adios* and departed toward our agreed rendezvous.

Chapter 18
The Captain Confronts Me Again

Arriving at our rendezvous about midday we carefully selected a sequestered spot some little distance from the busy highway, and there we rested, and ate our meals, and chatted cheerily as the sunlit hours crept lazily by.

Gradually the daylight faded and the evening closed in upon us while we sat there waiting and listening for the approach of Detriño's cavalcade.

Intense darkness had already gathered over the countryside before we heard the welcome rumble of the approaching oil trollies. On they came, jolting along over the ruts and rubbish of the rough country road, the cattle's head-bells jingling and the drivers' whips cracking in chorus. On they came, six oxen-drawn cradles, each one carrying a huge earthenware *tinaja* of oil slung low between the solid wooden wheels.

The foreman, as soon as he arrived, came up to me and asked for my instructions. My instructions, happily for all of us, were equally pleasant to him and to me, for as I was now particularly desirous of being left alone with my oil for a few moments, I gave the foreman a silver piece and told him to take his five men to the little wayside *vino* across the road and there drink a draught of wine to our health and prosperity.

Immediately after the men had gone I bade Ana go and strip my mule and bring all the cash and valuables to me. Then I removed the large cork bungs from my three oil jars and dropped the Doña Rosa's three hundred gold pieces into one jar and her jewels equally into the other two.

No sooner had I completed this device than three horsemen came galloping along the road from the direction of Burgos. One of them drew near to our cavalcade and lustily inquired for the leader of the party.

"O'ho! There, O'ho! There," he shouted as he drew near to the light of my lantern. "Who leads this company?"

Quietly I bade the women slip away up the side road. Then, drawing my hat well over my eyes, I ran forward to accept the challenge. "Here am I, Señor. It is I who leads this company," I shouted. "I, Pablo Acedo, oil merchant of Tolosa, at your service."

The man who had called me drew his rein and, as he passed between me and the dim light of the *vino*, I discerned the burly form and fearless face of the Captain of the Inquisition Guard, and my judgment was confirmed by the bandages he wore over the head wounds that I had given him during our recent fight on the road to Cabezón. The Captain had evidently missed us at Dueñasaeros, whence we had escaped several hours before he arrived, and he was now hunting for us along the Burgos road. He looked searchingly at me and asked whence I had come and where I was going.

In reply I raised my lantern and, keeping it well behind my face, I showed him my receipted account for the oil. I told him that my men were refreshing themselves in the wine shop yonder and that they would soon be joining me and we should then start away and travel through the night to Burgos. Thereupon he demanded sharply; "Did you pass two women as you came along the Villavieja road? They were on horseback and were carrying a great deal of luggage."

To this I tersely replied, "No, we did not encounter any strangers this afternoon."

My answer seemed to perplex him, but, being satisfied with my sincerity and my credentials, he hurried away with his companions to continue his futile search for us along the main road back again toward Dueñasaeros.

Chapter 19
Midnight on the Burgos Road

gleam of light now shone out from the *Vino* and spread like a yellow fan upon the road through the opening door as Detriño's men emerged from the warmth and comfort of the inn. The three unnecessary drivers were sent home, and my mule and the Captain's horse were haltered to the rear of our cavalcade. Then away we rumbled into the darkness, each of us seated upon the shaft of our respective trollies. On, and on, hour after hour doggedly and solidly pursuing our tedious way through the oppressive quietness of the lonely countryside. On and on we rumbled and jolted until midnight, when suddenly the road zig-zagged down into a deep ravine from the sides of which there arose a dense forest of cork trees. Down this we backed and zig-zagged into the rough ravine until we reached the dry bed of a river that traverses the valley. Just as we were about to cross it, however, the driver of the leading trolly in front of us drew his oxen to a standstill and shouted "*Cuidado*—Look out!" and, in an instant the whole cavalcade came to a sudden halt. Flickering lights now began to appear here and there in the forest and presently two armed men sprang toward us from among the trees. Peremptorily they bade us all get down and stand in a group together, while a third desperado advanced to the trollies and ransacked our bundles. After having searched our luggage for plunder he then returned to us individually and relieved us of the paltry cash that we had upon our persons!

Having thus speedily and successfully accomplished their coup, they retired to the rear of the cavalcade and there, two of them mounted the Captain's horse and the third bandit appropriated my faithful little mule. The three rascals jauntily departed, and waving us a courteous *Adios* as they went, they left us to pursue our journey in peace, poorer in pelf but richer in our experience of the ways of Spanish travel.

So once again we started on our cheerless journey and lumbered up and up the further side of the steep-set tortuous ravine until we emerged once more into the open country. Then pressing forward with the utmost speed we could exact from our oxen, we jolted and lumbered along the dark and difficult road toward the great city of Burgos. On and on we journeyed, sleepily and numbed in the bitter cold and cheerless silence until the darkness gradually lifted and the hesitating twilight of the dawn crept timidly up the eastern sky and revealed to us the first faint outlines of the cathedral spires of the distant city shining like phantoms in the morning mist.

While I was gazing and meditating upon the tender beauty of the scene that rose before me, my reverie was interrupted by the Doña Rosa. She had leapt down from her seat on the shaft of the trolley behind me and had run forward to overtake me.

The pale sunlight of the early morning shone softly upon her upturned face and emphasized her gladsome beauty as, with unwonted geniality and gratitude, she looked up into my face and thanked me for my forethought in securing the safety of her fortune at the bottom of our precious oil jars!

In joyful response to this token of her increasing trustfulness, I looked down earnestly into her merry eyes, and said: "*Muchisimas gracias*, my beloved mistress—many many thanks for your kind appreciation: and now may I pray you to believe that henceforward my only joy and quest in life shall be to make you prosperous and happy."

"*Señora*," I continued as I looked intently into her merry eyes, "*Señora*, did you notice how intensely dark was the hour that preceded the splendor of the dawn? It is always so; it is Nature's ordered and significant way, and to those bereaved and sorrowing souls who can discern the signs and promises of Heaven it is a never-failing harbinger of hope—for it is always the blackest hour in life that precedes the dawn of a brighter and a happier day.

"Look, my beloved mistress, look at the glorious sunrise yonder. Is it not significant of the promises of Heaven? Is it not a harbinger of returning joy to you? And yet, *Señora*, I have sometimes heard you say, 'The dead do not return!' But look, my beloved mistress, look how majestically the returning sun ascends above those eastern spires, and yet it was only yesterday that he seemed to die and vanish in the fires of the evening sky!"

We were now drawing near to the Puerta Santa Maria—that noble bastion that guards the entrance to Burgos. Presently, as we proceeded, we crossed the bridge that spans the river and halted beneath the deep, windswept gateway. There our papers and merchandise were examined and customs-dues exacted. Then away we jolted up the narrow *calle* that ascends to the east side of the Cathedral, and there, at a busy oil store in the Plaza de Santa Maria, we delivered Detriño's three *tinajas* of the second quality oil that his Burgos customer had ordered.

As soon as that task was completed, I asked Detriño's foreman if he knew of a small shop in Burgos that I could rent as a branch of my Tolosa business and where I could deposit my three *tinajas* of first quality oil. The foreman keen to oblige, or maybe to earn a commission, promptly introduced me to the landlord of a vacant store nearby and for this store and the two dwelling rooms above it, the landlord (thanks to my being one of Detriño's customers) at once accepted me as a tenant without making any further inquiries concerning me. An agreement was promptly drawn by an attorney who attested my signature and gave me an acknowledgement for a month's rent which I paid in advance.

Thus, before midday, I the erstwhile *buhonero* had now established myself as Pablo Acedo, an accredited oil merchant, in the city of Burgos!

Yes, within a week I had advanced my worldly status from that of a ragged *buhonero* to the position of courier, and now today, I had advanced myself still further in the social scale to the status of a merchant in one of Spain's most flourishing cities.

My beloved, too, had similarly advanced herself from the lowly condition of a farmer's wife to the dignity of a French gentlewoman travelling with her maid. And now, at last, she had unconsciously rehearsed her heart's desire—and mine—and had acknowledged to Detriño and the world that she was the wife of Pablo Acedo, alias the courier alias Timoteo Pereño and alias Don Fernando de la Mina!

But O! how indignant she was at my presumptuous jest, and how coldly she received my attempts at humour! But then, how little did my beloved suspect that the farce we were then rehearsing was so prophetic of our anticipated joy!

Chapter 20

Rome's Resurgent Power

Our little home at Burgos was most pleasantly situated, for it overlooked the eastern end of the glorious cathedral.

During the first week of our residence there we were as happy as our sadly altered lot would allow us to be. I sold oil, the Doña Rosa arranged and presided over our home, and Ana did the marketing and waited upon us. Our erstwhile enemies seemed to have quite lost track of us, and it now appeared likely that, if we remained at Burgos just a little while longer, we should establish a new identity and thus be able, for business reasons, to travel unmolested and un-challenged to the northern limits of Spain and pass into Protestant Navarre before the winter was upon us.

Toward the end of the first week I began to feel sure that at last our enemies had really abandoned pursuit of us. But at the same time, I be-gan to suspect that a new enemy had arisen in our own household—a new enemy that threatened to wreck our safety. An enemy in our very midst that none of us had suspected—a spiritual enemy!

Now, my son, in the course of my observations of men and women I have invariably noticed that old associations and customs lay a stron-ger hold on women than on men. In the sensitive matter of religion, for instance, it is the woman and not the man who clings longest to an old and outworn faith.

The New Lutheran Truth that made me perfectly and permanently free from the old superstitious fears that Rome delights to create in her adherents, and henceforth my only anxiety—my constant anxiety in tranquility and in danger—was, "How shall I be able to escape with my beloved from Spain to safety?"

But not so your mother. She was not so easily liberated from the old religious thralldom.

Whether it was the fancied call of conscience or whether it was the constant beholding of the reverential loveliness of the cathedral, or the insistent invite of the sacramental bell, or the fond remembrance of the spiritual comfort that the Roman Church had hitherto ministered to her pure and noble soul, whatever it was that caused her longings I do not know. But it happened that, after we had resided at Burgos only a week, your mother, by some fell influence, developed a desire—a sacred desire—that threatened to imperil us all. She craved to attend the ordinance of Confession in the cathedral that afternoon at three o'clock, so that she might receive the Holy Sacrament next day.

In vain I argued that it would be too perilous! I urged, too, that Confession must be made to God and that a priestly mediator is unnecessary. I urged that the Divine Presence in a spiritual presence vouchsafed exclusively "neither in this mountain nor yet at Jerusalem," but anywhere and at any time to the true worshiper who worships the Father in spirit and in truth. The presence of the Body and Blood of Christ I reverently admitted to be a mystery beyond the reach of human ken; but I pleaded that Scripture, justice, and common sense forbade us to believe that the material and spiritual Presence of Christ can be commanded by a miracle performed by the celebrant at the altar!

But it was all in vain that I argued and pleaded with my beloved. She was possessed and obsessed with a deep and earnest craving for religious comfort, and it was this pious and determined desire of hers that threatened to completely wreck our hard-won safety.

It was three o'clock, and my beloved was descending into the store, prepared to walk across the cathedral.

It was three o'clock, and I was determined, at all costs, to prevent her.

Firmly, but courteously, I intercepted her way at the foot of the stairs and requested her to enter the sitting room. There, standing before her with my back to the door, I said:

"Señora, your safety compels me to prevent you from going to Confession. I would that I could persuade you to overcome your desire. Have you considered that, before you can receive priestly absolution, you must confess your every transgression of thought and deed against the authority and teaching of the Church? Will you, Señora—will you, reveal to the priest that you are a renegade—a student and adherent of the Reformed Lutheran Faith, and that you are evading arrest for heresy? Will you tell him that you are prepared to recant your heresy and curse your betrothal to Don Fernando de la Mina? The priest, perhaps, will tell you that the soul of Don Fernando is suffering the torments of Hell—maybe! But you know, in your heart of hearts, you know that God is just and merciful and that His love is infinite and eternal. Believe me, my beloved mistress, Don Fernando is safe in God's most gracious keeping and is now patiently and faithfully awaiting you in love that has been intensified and purified in sorrow. In his name, and in his spirit, and by the love he bore you and bears you still, I plead with you, Señora, do not betray yourself and him—Oh, do not weep, Señora! Your grief breaks my heart, for as loyal servant I am compelled to hurt you, but as a servant, alas! I cannot comfort you. Trust Ana and trust me to guard you and bring you into safety and I will promise you that ere your year of grace is passed you shall—if you so desire—receive the Benediction of the Church—the Church that you have served so faithfully and which has requited you and your loved one so unmercifully!"

She seemed not to hear me but sat silently weeping, weeping, while I, her betrothed—my heart wrung with compassion—was compelled to stand apart, unable to soothe or comfort her. And so I let her weep until the passion passed and a more reasonable state of mind possessed her.

Then she arose and looked intently and almost pleadingly into my face. She looked into my eyes, she looked at my ears and forehead. Her eyes looked down at my hands, and I detected a repressed and unspoken inquiry of surprise gradually suffuse her quickened countenance. But all too soon the tender and pathetic beauty of it faded away as the cruel certainty of my death dispelled the momentary joy that my likeness had awakened in her heart.

For some moments she was sad and silent. Then she thanked me, somewhat imperiously, for my counsel and said: "Señor, I already owe my life and all that I now possess to your wisdom and courage; I will never imperil you and Ana. No! Not even to gratify the most sacred desires of my heart. Don Fernando de la Mina died as a heretic and a martyr to what he and I believe to be the Truth. Henceforth, whether it please God to deliver me from this present peril or to abandon me to the fires of the dreadful Auto de Fé, I will live and die in spiritual fellowship with my noble and ..."

Chapter 21
Foiled!

She suddenly stopped speaking and fled from me, shrieking with terror, behind the curtain that screened my bed at the further end of the room.

She was already terribly overwrought, and now the unexpected sight of Father Lorenzo's malignant visage, as he stepped stealthily into the room, completely shattered her self-control.

Quick as thought I passed behind the priest and barred his exit. But Father Lorenzo, heedless of my action, advanced to my bed recess and withdrawing the curtain, said, very quietly and persuasively: "Have no fear, daughter. The Holy Church will be gracious to you. I overheard all your conversation, and I appreciate your religious cravings. Have no fear, daughter. The Holy Church will be gracious to you and you shall receive again the comfort that you crave—the comfort that the Church alone can give—and you shall yet work for and win her clemency for the release of Don Fernando's soul."

For a while Doña Rosa stood motionless, like a fascinated, frightened bird before a snake, gazing helplessly upon the evil face of her destroyer.

Presently, recovering herself a little, she asked, very softly and very penitently: "Father, how were you led to discover my retreat?"

"By the inspiration of God," he replied, "by the inspiration of God I was led into the marketplace this afternoon, and, there, seeing your maid purchasing fruit at one of the stores, I waited and followed her to your home."

"O'ho!" thought I, "so this discovery is accidental, and is known only to Father Lorenzo—and the Captain of the Inquisition Guard, as yet, ignorant of our present hiding place!"

Being now assured on this point I determined to keep Father Lorenzo from communicating with the Captain. So I instantly stepped back and deliberately fastened the door.

"That," said the priest, turning around on me as he heard the movement of the bolt, "that is quite useless, sirah! The Doña Rosa is known to be in Burgos, and her arrest is inevitable whether you attempt to delay me or not."

"*Delay* you, Father Lorenzo!" I replied, angrily. "*Delay* you forsooth! I do not intend to *delay* you. I bolted that door because I intend to kill you and to avenge by your death the martyrdom of Don Carlos de Seso, whom you impeached, and Don Juan de Lario, whom you have trapped, and Don Fernando de la Mina, whose life you blasted, and the thousand other innocent victims whom you have harried and persecuted with your subtle brutality. Delay you forsooth! No, no, Father Lorenzo, I do not intend to delay you. I intend to kill you! So prepare yourself to die." Then, drawing my rapier, I pressed its point upon his chest.

Father Lorenzo heard me in unperturbed silence; then, after facing me calmly for a moment, he lifted the crucifix from his girdle, kissed it and prayed—or seemed to pray—silently and fervently, and then said: " Now, sirah, if you dare to lay hands upon the Lord's anointed, strike—and strike deep!"

"No, No!" screamed the Doña Rosa, as she sprang forward and flung herself between the priest and me, and thus diverted my rapier from him and separated us far apart. "Father," pleaded my beloved, as she now knelt submissively before the priest, "Father, I will return with you."

Astonished and baffled by this unexpected fatal self-surrender on the part of my beloved I, too, reconsidered my murderous decision, and humbly fell upon my knees before the priest, saying: "Father, forgive my sudden insanity and grant me your pardon and your blessing!"

A triumphant and contemptuous smile suffused the subtle countenance of the priest as he stood and looked down upon his two kneeling conquests! But the smile was quickly suppressed as he gazed upon my penitent countenance. Slowly and authoritatively he strode forward and stood before me to grant me his forgiveness and his blessing. But, before he could spread his hands over my head or utter a single word, I suddenly gripped his knees and hurled him backward with a vigorous thrust of my head. The blow completely doubled him up, and he fell heavily upon the floor.

Just at that moment Ana knocked at the door of the room to ascertain the reason of the commotion!

I quickly unbolted the door and admitted her. Then calling upon her to assist me, we secured the priest hand and foot and bound him tightly to my bed.

Instant flight was once more imperative for, although the priest lay harmless on the bed, I knew that he would soon be missed and sought for. It was, therefore, necessary that we should make our escape and get away as far as possible before Father Lorenzo should be discovered in the vacated home of Pablo Acedo the—as yet—unsuspected oil merchant of Burgos! So I, at once, sent the women upstairs to pack while I locked up my store and hurried to the *Judería* (the Jew's quarter), and there I purchased, among other things, a couple of well-worn workmen's suits. Bringing these home with me, I bade my beloved and Ana disguise themselves in them while I recovered the money and valuables that still lay in safety at the bottom of our oil jars. These I dropped, all together, into one medium-sized flagon of oil, and this I now took with me down to the city gate.

While I arrived at the gate, I stood there for a little while chatting pleasantly with the officers of the guard. I had anticipated some such emergency as this, and therefore, as Pablo Acedo, I had prudently established and maintained friendly relations with the customs officers during our brief stay at Burgos.

After chatting with them for a few moments, I inquired if any of the officers had seen two of my workmen recently pass through the gates.

"No," they replied.

Then, with seeming annoyance at my workmen's delay, I asked if they would allow me to leave my flagon of oil in the guardroom while I went back to seek my men. To this casual and reasonable request they good-naturedly agreed, and thereupon, I left my oil flagon, with its precious contents, in their safe custody while I sped back to my store in the Plaza de Santa Maria. Then, within a quarter of an hour, I returned to the city gate accompanied by my two workmen.

After chatting for a little while with the friendly guard, we three men with our precious oil jar and our several bundles bade a sincere *adios* to the obliging officers and after merrily exchanging greetings with them as we went, we were allowed to pass unchallenged and un-suspected through the narrow and carefully guarded gateway of Puerta Santa Maria!

But how grimly our forced merriment mocked our insistent fear and anxiety. We knew only too well that a single incautious word or action on the part of any one of us would betray us to certain death for—proscribed as we were by the all-powerful Roman Catholic Church we had—*ipso facto*—become outcasts from the social and religious world, and henceforward, the hand of every Spaniard was against us.

We had already traveled one hundred miles from Valladolid. One hundred miles! And yet, despite our devious course and rapid change of disguise, we had only just managed to escape arrest on three occasions: first at Cabezón, then at Dueñasaeros, and now at Burgos! To-morrow, or perhaps tonight, Father Lorenzo would be discovered and set at liberty. Then he would, at once, institute inquiries and would quickly find out that Doña Rosa and her maid, together with a third companion, had passed through the Puerta Santa Maria that very af-ternoon, disguised as three workmen. Then the Captain of the Inquisition Guard would be immediately instructed to press his pursuit of us further northward toward the Pyrénées which was now the only way we could travel toward liberty.

We were now, indeed, in a desperate plight, and it was necessary that we should make the utmost of our present start and speedily place as long a distance as possible between Burgos and our next resting place.

Chapter 22
Three French Farmers

How long it was that Father Lorenzo lay undiscovered upon my bed I do not know, but I do know—and I remember it with gratitude—that while he lay there undisturbed I and my workmen passed safely through the gates and round the city walls of Burgos until we reached the Great North Road. There, through the long hours of the night, we lay in our cloaks by the open roadside and rested, as best we could, until the early morning. Then between four and five o'clock, we hailed and boarded the quick traveling wagon that plies between Burgos and Briviesca—a town about thirty miles to the north of the Cathedral City. Arriving at Briviesca, we at once boarded another vehicle and continued our journey thirty-five miles further northward to Vittoria. There, feeling sure that we had now shaken the pursuers off our track, for at least a few days, we prepared to remain for a while in order to rest and establish a totally different identity among the Spanish Basques.

It was nearly midnight when we arrived at Vittoria. The *galera*—the country wagon that conveyed us—drew up in the patio of the Fonda Brettaja in order to set down the local passengers and also to change its team of ten mules before starting again on the next stage of its journey. We three "men" alighted in the courtyard of the inn, stiff and cramped with the cold and the discomfort of our tedious day's traveling.

As soon as I had alighted at the Fonda I at once approached the kindly landlord and learned from him the Fonda Brettaja was the favorite rendezvous of farmers and seed merchants of the district. Having ascertained this useful piece of information, I promptly informed the landlord that I and my two friends were three French farmers who had come into the Spanish Basque country to buy seed.

In order to establish this reputation and, at the same time to glean as much knowledge as possible concerning our new calling—we "three farmers" frequently visited the market in Campillo Susso, and during the next few days there we soon became acquainted with several of the resident Basque merchants.

One of these traders was Chaggara Ydharro, a genial and interesting man who, on learning that we intended soon to return to France, offered to afford me an introduction to his nephew at Tolosa (Tolosa is a Basque town about forty miles further north), and he invited me to call upon his nephew as we passed through the town on our homeward journey. This nephew, whose name was Dara Ydharro, was, so the uncle told us, a merchant who traded with his Basque relatives in Navarre, just across the Pyrénées.

This timely information keenly interested me, for the winter was fast approaching, and it was, therefore, expedient that we should make our attempt to cross into Protestant Navarre before the snow should block the mountain passes. So I determined that we would leave Vittoria next day by mules for Tolosa, where I would at once seek Chaggara's nephew and endeavor to profit by his acquaintance.

I already knew, however, that the Basques were among the staunchest of Catholics, but I thought and hoped that, in spite of this, I might perhaps be able to utilize the young Basque merchant's assistance in order to facilitate our escape from Spain.

With this hopeful prospect in view we decided that this should be our last night at hospitable Vittoria. But it turned out to be a very perilous one for us, for it so happened that while we French and Spanish Basque farmers were sitting together at the supper table, three Spaniards entered the Fonda and came and joined our company—the Captain of the Inquisition Guard, an officer, and Father Lorenzo!

Alas! They had failed to find us at Briviesca and were now pressing their pursuit of us further and further north. They could not by any means have been informed of our retreat at Vittoria, nor could they have been informed of our new disguises, and it would seem to have been nothing but sheer ill-fortune that had directed them here to the Fonda Brettaja just on the very eve of our departure!

The three Spaniards sat deedily together at the end of the table—a little group by themselves. There they sat, speaking quietly in their native Castilian in the midst of the loud and musical, but to them and to us quite unintelligible, babble of Basque tongues that kept up a continual chorus at our end of the table.

During supper time I stole covert glances at our pursuers, and I was thankful to observe that neither the Captain nor his subordinate recognized us. But I was certain that Father Lorenzo suspected me! And, surely enough, immediately after supper, he arose slowly from the table and came cautiously toward me. He was, as I have already told you, a short, sturdily built man, with eyes and eyebrows nearly as dark as those of my beloved, and his face wore a womanly expression that was unnatural and deceptive.

When I saw that he was approaching me I stood perfectly still and waited for him where I was standing by the rain-water well in the center of the patio.

I was alone for I had already warned my two "farmer" friends to go up to their bedroom and remain there out of sight.

Father Lorenzo approached me slowly and, as it were, casually. Then smiling benignly, he said: "*Buenas noches, hijo mio!–habla usted Castellano?* Good evening, my Son! Do you speak the Spanish Language?"

"*Muy poco, Padre, muy poco.* Very little, Father, very little," I replied, speaking with a decided foreign accent and at the same time raising my shoulders with a French shrug.

The Father thereupon scrutinized my face, and then, pretending not to recognize me, he turned unconcernedly away.

I was now quite certain he knew me. But happily I was also certain of another fact—I knew that the Captain of the Inquisition Guard had failed to recognize me. Therefore I determined, at all costs, to prevent the priest from communicating with the Captain while we three made our escape from Vittoria that night. So, secretly—as it were—secretly taking a tablet from my purse, I wrote a few lines upon it and then stepped cautiously with it across the patio to the corner where the ostler stood—and Father Lorenzo watched me!

"José," said I, speaking rather softly to the ostler—and Father Lorenzo drew near and listened, his lips moving the while as if he were absorbed in prayer! "José," said I, "at what time will the mules be ready for us in the morning?"

"At eight o'clock, Señor" he replied—for that was the time we had arranged with him for us to depart on mule-back for Tolosa.

"Thank you, José," said I. Then handed him the note that Father Lorenzo had seen me write and said rather quietly, but just loud enough for Father Lorenzo to hear: "José, I want you to take this note to the Casa Deneda in the Calle Reina Isabel, and I will wait here for you to bring me the Señora's reply."

Father Lorenzo fell right into the trap, for, presently as I looked from my bedroom down into the courtyard, I saw José start upon his fool's errand, and then, a few moments afterwards, I saw the priest follow him at a discreet distance—thus evidently expecting to discover the hiding place of the Doña Rosa and her maid.

Ah! The Holy Office was grimly determined to capture my beloved. She was a victim worth spending time and money upon, and, in order to achieve their end, they spared neither pains nor expense, because the Riello estate would prove rich plunder for the Church.

But, my son, I ought here, perhaps, to explain to you that by the law of Spain—despite the tremendous power of the Inquisition—the Church herself has no power of confiscation. She must first arraign and convict her prisoner of heresy and then the process of the law confiscates and conveys the plunder to the Church. But, unhappily for the Church, if Doña Rosa should be able to escape from Spain, and thus abandon and forfeit her property, the whole of the plunder would then fall exclusively to the State—as no charge of heresy could, in her absence, be successfully preferred against her.

So I watched the eager priest pass through the wicket into the darkness and then I hurried to the women's room and bade them pack the luggage and hasten away with it by themselves as best they could to the Venta (the small inn) in the Calle Enita. There I told them they were to wait for the midnight *galera* that would take them direct to Tolosa.

I also arranged that I would follow them to the Venta a little later on and travel with them if I could—but I would not risk accompanying them now, lest by any inadvertency my association with them should betray their identity. But I impressed upon them that willy-nilly, they must travel to Tolosa by the midnight *galera* with or without me, for I was doubtful whether I should succeed in evading both the Captain and the priest, now that the priest was certain of my identity.

Chapter 23

The Lay-Brother

After the women had started on their way to the Venta, I waited a few minutes on the deserted patio in order to make quite sure that no one was following them. Then I, too, passed unobserved, or so I thought, through the little wicket and cautiously stepped into the dark, narrow roadway. The night was dark but I could just see the women about a hundred yards ahead of me. They had already reached the end of the street and were now entering the wide *plaza* at the further end of the *calle*. So I drew my cloak closely around me and walked rapidly after them. I had not proceeded many paces, however, when I heard the soft footsteps of someone following me.

"Was it the priest?" thought I. Had he seen through my trickery and gone out—not to follow the ostler but to wait for me and then follow me to the Doña Rosa's real retreat? Was it the priest who was following me now—or was it someone else—someone perhaps quite unconcerned with me or my doings?

In my uncertainty I continued to walk on briskly. Then, suddenly I stood still and waited—so did my pursuer!

Now the position of affairs at this crisis was so critical that I dared not risk any uncertainty, so I again walked quickly forward, and then suddenly turned back and stood face to face—not with Father Lorenzo—but with his servant, the fat lay-brother with whom I had fraternized at Dueñasaeros!

Fool that I was! I had completely forgotten that smug rascal. Of course I had not seen him at the Fonda during the evening, because he had supped in the servants' room. Thus I had carelessly failed to number him among our enemies.

The fat lay-brother halted and stood complacently beaming upon me! Dullard that he was he seemed to be quite unabashed at being caught spying. He greeted me with a saucy smirk and a "hallo Frenchy," to which I angrily replied, in good colloquial Castellano, "*Que bajo perillo!* You dirty dog! Why are you following me?"

"Because I am ordered to do so," he blandly replied.

"Then," said I, "you will have a very long walk tonight, if you obey your orders," and thereupon I turned on my heels and hastened away up to the square, and stood there waiting at the corner of the Calle Enita until I saw my women safely enter the Venta. Then, just as the lay-brother came panting to my side I started off again and, gradually quickening my pace to a good six miles an hour, I began to pilot my portly companion several times round the town. Off we went across the square, then down the hill to the city gate. Then round the walls to the Campillo Susso and under the shadows of St. Miguel. On and on we went breathlessly past the College and up again to the plaza. Then in and out among the twisted byways and back again to the gates and then round the city walls once more!—I, slim and youthful, enjoying the exhilarating exercise—he, of middle age and more than middle weight, puffing and perspiring behind me—now lagging and now making furtive little spurts in his vain endeavor to keep close to my heels. From nine o'clock to nearly eleven I kept the faithful hound in full run! But still he stuck to me. Then I increased my pace still further and finally I began to sprint—but even this vigorous effort failed to shake him off.

So I returned to the *plaza* and there resolved to rest contentedly till midnight when I intended, by a belated rush, to overtake and board the *galera* when it was well started on its way, and there leave the panting lay-brother choused and lonely in the deserted roadway!

With that delightful project in view, I now sat down complacently in the middle of the square with my back to one of the trees; and the wet and weary lay-brother slithered gratefully down beside me. I buckled up my cloak to the throat and settled myself very contentedly, for I knew that just so long as the lay-brother remained with me just so long would Father Lorenzo, after his own fruitless quest, continue to wait at the Fonda for the return of his servant.

The portly brother chortled and puffed as he shuffled himself in an easy position beside me. Then, nudging my arm and laughing inanely at his own silly wit he said: "Frenchy, by the way you walk and run, you must have been a most excellent courier!"

I did not answer the fool!

"*Amigo mio,*" he persisted. "Tell me, I pray, by what good fortune did you rise so speedily from courier to gentleman, eh?"

But still I refused to talk and, presently, the portly brother yawned. Then he yawned again—and again—and thus in the frozen silence the weary moments dragged slowly on. The church bell tolled the departure of each tedious quarter of an hour. Half past ten, a quarter to eleven, half past eleven and then the quarter to twelve chime boomed and quivered and died in the night air. Then in the succeeding silence I was made orally conscious that my boon companion was soundly and sonorously asleep!

I rose quietly from my alfresco resting place and went across the plaza and walked down the Calle Enita a little way. Then, seeing a light approaching me, I hastily stepped into the shadow of an archway just as the night watchman with his lantern came shuffling by. This animated old bundle of rags—topped with a pointed *sombrero* and draped in a long tattered cloak—went slowly past me, staff and lantern in hand. Then he walked into the plaza and stood there, right in the middle of the square where the poor lay-brother was peacefully sleeping, and there, raising his head and his voice, the night watchman yelled out: "*La media noche y sereno!* Twelve o'clock and a very fine night!"

This sudden, raucous announcement completely shattered my late companion's dreams and woke him up with a start!

I watched him from my point of vantage in the shaded archway and saw him sit up, rub his eyes, and look around him in idiotic bewilderment. Then he stood up and, rubbing his eyes again, he peered successively down each of the turnings that branched away from the plaza. Failing to see me in any of the streets, he now began to look behind the several trees and then into all the doorways around the square, but nowhere could he find a trace of "Frenchy." Then, at last, failing to discover anyone else abroad but the watchman, and now evidently despairing of ever seeing "Frenchy" again, he set off back to the Fonda Brettaja there to report his failure to his equally unfortunate master, while I was jovially assisting the women with their bundles into the strawstrewn *galera* and departing with them in safety from Vittoria on our forty-mile night journey northward to Tolosa.

Chapter 24

Dara Ydharro

Early next morning the clumsy old hooded wagon jolted noisily into the great square of Tolosa. Immediately upon our arrival, I inquired for the home of Dara Ydharro, and at once proceeded there in order to present my letter of introduction.

Fortunately for us young Dara Ydharro was at home when I called. When I handed him his uncle's letter he welcomed me as cordially as if I had been an old friend. Happily, for me, Ydharro was fairly fluent in the Spanish language, for, as I have already told you, I did not and do not understand a word of the Basque tongue, which seems to me to have no relation whatever with either French or Castellano.

Young Dara Ydharro's straightforward, business-like appearance pleased me at first sight, and, being thus encouraged, I sought and obtained from him the accommodation of a couple of rooms in his house—one for myself and one for my two farmer friends.

Ydharro was a quiet man of the good peasant type—tall, lissome, with clear blue eyes and jet-black hair—and I felt confident that we should soon become close friends. Gradually, as I began to feel more sure of my ground, I told him that we three farmers desired to return to our native France as soon as possible; and one day, soon after we had taken up residence with him, I hinted that we had brought with us a quantity of gunpowder and some small arms which we intended to smuggle into Navarre en route. This little bit of smuggling, I confessed, presented us with some difficulty, especially as we were foreigners, and I suggested our willingness to pay liberally for any assistance that would enable my friends and me to take our contraband merchandise across the Pyrénéen frontier without having to traverse any of the guarded passes.

I felt perfectly safe in making this overture because, from previous observation, I felt pretty sure that Ydharro, himself, had illicit dealings with his friends and relatives across the frontier in Navarre. I had noticed, for instance, that he was recently away from home for a couple of nights, and that on the morning of his return he was very busy in his barn unloading goods that had certainly never arrived there in the daylight!

Ydharro was a typical Basque peasant. Brave—but superstitious. A fighter for freedom and yet, at the same time, a devout son of the Roman Catholic Church. He was generous in spirit and scrupulous in matters of personal honour, but strangely enough he was, at the same time, frankly proud of his prosperity as a *contrabandista*!

"You see, my friends, we Basques are a difficult people to understand. Our code of honour and many of our customs are distinctly and racially our own. We Basques are a nationality to ourselves. We are neither French nor Spanish, and our home is on both sides of the Pyrénées—both sides! This land was ours long before the *Gauls* were a people. It was ours centuries before the Iberians set foot in Spain. The stern mountain barrier that separates France from Spain does not separate the French and Spanish Basques. It only serves to unite us in one common alliance. For we Basques of Spain and our brother Basques of French Navarre mutually help each other to plunder both the Spaniard, whom we call the '*Chucurra*,' and the Frenchman, whom we call '*Gabacho*.' I mean no offense, to you, my friends.

"Well," he continued, "it may interest you to know that there is a safe smugglers' track to and from Navarre. It is near the Pyrénéen Pass of the Puerta de Maya, which is about forty miles from here. This smuggling track is known only to me and my family. We have used it safely and profitably for several generations and, if you are prepared to pay for assistance to get your contraband free of duty into Navarre, I daresay I can manage the matter for you."

Without further parley we four men pledged ourselves to secrecy and then we struck a bargain whereby Ydharro undertook to escort me and my two friends from Tolosa to Maya and from thence across the Spanish frontier into Navarre for the sum of three hundred *reales*—one hundred and fifty to be paid at Maya and the balance when we reached Navarre.

We decided to make our departure for Maya early the following day, and, as it happened, it was none too soon, for while I was dressing next morning I chanced to look down into the street and there, just beneath my window, I saw Father Lorenzo in earnest conversation with Ydharro! Had our Basque friend turned traitor? I could not believe it. But believe it or not, one thing was quite certain. This interview between Ydharro and Father Lorenzo could hardly have been accidental! But whether the interview was due to chance or treachery was all the same to me, for it only proved one thing, viz., that our pursuers had again discovered our track and would soon be pressing in upon us.

So I hurried downstairs eager to depart. The mules were quickly saddled and we were soon on our way to Maya.

Throughout the early and middle part of that day we pressed on as hard as we could. Then, during the afternoon, as we were riding across the undulating country toward Maya, I suddenly asked Ydharro: "What was your business with that priest this morning?"

To which he replied quite frankly: "As I was returning home from early Mass this morning that priest overtook me and inquired if I had seen the three French farmers who, he said, had recently come into the town from Vittoria, and I told him that you were lodging in my house and that I was taking you to Maya today."

"And did you tell him that you had bargained to smuggle us and our contraband into Navarre by your secret track?"

"Certainly I did," he replied. "The Holy Church, as you know, does not forbid our business of smuggling."

In light of this alarming revelation I fell to reckoning our chance of escape. The priest, I knew, could not personally arrest us. Our arrest would have to be effected under legal authority by the Captain of the Inquisition Guard. Therefore, before we could be arrested, Father Lorenzo would have to send for the Captain to Vittoria, or perhaps to Burgos or even to Valldolid. That, certainly, was much in our favor; but was that gain of time sufficient for our escape? Should we be able to escape into Navarre before the Captain could arrive at Maya? Obviously our only chance of safety now lay in a speedy escape across the frontier by Ydharro's secret track before the priest or the Captain could prevent us.

"Ydharro," said I, "when do you intend to cross the frontier?"

"Well," he replied, with slow, complacent calculation, "we shall cross immediately when the moon is sufficiently high. That may, perhaps, be tomorrow week, or it may be that even then we shall have to wait a day or two for a clear night. But," he continued encouragingly, "that need not disturb you or your companions, for at Maya you will be among congenial friends and perfectly safe from spies or any risk of arrest."

"Safe from spies," forsooth, "or any risk of arrest?" Why! What with Father Lorenzo and his servant already in touch with us and the Captain of the Guard already on our heels, we shall be beset with the most cunning and inveterate of spies and in the direst risk of arrest. But for all my misgiving I had, of course, to appear content with Ydharro's assurance of our prospective safety. But, at the same, time, I was determined to be secretly prepared to take advantage of any and every opportunity of escape that might arise in the development of our anxious circumstances.

Chapter 25
A Council of War at Maya

L ate that night we arrived at Maya, the wretched little Pyrénéen village that nestles, or rather crouches, in the deep ravine that leads up to the Puerta de Maya, that majestic but forbidding granite gateway that guards this lonely exit from Spain.

On our arrival at Maya we rode our mules into the patio of the "Parador Choria"– which is the Basque for "the Bird Inn"–and there, before retiring for the night, I gave young Dara Ydharro the one hundred and fifty *reales* that I promised to pay him on or safe arrival at Maya.

Next morning Ydharro introduced us to the *contrabandista* fraternity at the inn and elsewhere as three French business friends of his, and during our next few days of galling inactivity at Maya, he did his utmost to keep us patient and to set our anxieties at rest. He explained that on the first favorable night we four "men" with our sundry merchandise would all leave the inn together and start to walk up the *puerto* (the ravine), "as if," said he, "we were silly Gabachos or Chacurras and intended to pass through the Puerta de Maya and meekly pay the duty on our goods! But, you can rest assured my friends," said he laughingly, " that neither King Philip of Spain nor Queen Jeanne of Navarre has ever yet exacted tribute from Dara Ydharro, for, just about a mile this side of the Puerta, we shall enter a narrow cleft that is almost hidden in the ravine and up this we shall scramble for about forty or fifty feet. Then we shall pass in and out among the rocks almost immediately over the heads of the guileless custom officers at the frontier gate two hundred feet below. Then, by carefully traversing a narrow ledge of rock for another mile or so and dropping from boulder to boulder round the southern side of the Navarrois Gate, we shall follow a goat track down to a shepherd's hut, and thence through a cattle farm, from whence we shall emerge, my friends—we shall emerge—unplundered and unchallenged on the Queen's highway! Once there, my friend," said the jubilant *contrabandista*, "once there, you can sell your powder and small arms—or whatever you've brought – at a substantial profit without any awkward questions being asked."

And having delivered himself of this graphic forecast of our exploit, Ydharro laughed lightheartedly in anticipation of our success. I prudently joined in the laugh, but not lightheartedly, because one supremely anxious thought kept haunting me: "Shall we be able to get away from Maya before the Captain of the Inquisition Guard arrives?"

So while Yadharro gabbled on I quietly cudgeled my brains to devise some reasonable means of hastening his departure from Maya via his secret track. But failing this, I then thought that, I myself might perhaps, be able to find another secret and, as yet, undiscovered track over the mountains into Navarre. Why not? But I soon decided that such a virgin track was unlikely to exist near where so many smugglers worked. Then I endeavored to devise some means whereby we three "men" could remain somewhere in secret hiding unbeknown to the priest or the Captain, and there wait for Ydharro's leisurely crossing. But think how I would—the problem of our timely escape seemed almost insoluble.

One thing was certain—we could not hasten our departure by passing through the Puerta like three ordinary peasants or merchants. This was absolutely impossible because we had no conduct papers and no legitimate business with Navarre to explain away the real purpose of our departure. Neither could we pass through the gates as law-abiding civilians on pleasure bent, because this would provoke the inevitable search for contraband and would soon discover our cash and jewelry and thus arouse suspicion which would result in a fatal detention.

What should we do? Should we risk the attempt to pass through the Puerta or should we wait for the moon to light Ydharro's track? Truly, I was on the horns of desperate dilemma—for to attempt to pass through the gates was to risk almost certain detention—and arrest—while to wait for the moonlight was simply to wait for the Captain's warrant. So in my uncertainty I decided to call a council of war to consider this momentous question, and so, early in the evening of our fourth day at Maya, I invited Doña Rosa and Ana to come to my bedroom and there talk the matter over with me.

Now whilst we were talking together—or rather whispering—I fancied that I heard movements and the sounds of low conversation in Ydharro's bedroom, which was next to mine. So signaling to the women to be silent, I listened intently and then crept out on to the gallery. A light was in my neighbor's room, and it shone beneath the door and through the chink in the window shutter. Placing my ear near to the keyhole of the door I now distinctly heard my Basque neighbor speaking to another man.

"But," said he, "I did not know that they were heretics. I have taken their money, Father, and I have passed my word of honour to them."

"From these indiscretions I can absolve you, my son," replied the priest, "but from the sin of willful and persistent opposition to the commands of the Holy Church there can be no forgiveness. Therefore," continued the priest sternly, "I adjure you to depart at once and deliver this letter to the Captain of the Inquisition Guard at the monastery of San Salvador at Urdax" (a little town about five miles away.)

I stepped back quickly and crouched in the shadow of the gallery as Father Lorenzo, after abruptly leaving Ydharro, stepped out from the bedroom. His cassock brushed my face as he passed me in the darkness! Then he went down the stairs to the patio gate there to await the Basque's departure and thus make sure that his command would be obeyed.

Immediately after the priest had descended I hastened back to my room. Soon after I entered it we heard the sound of movements in the adjoining room. Then we heard a light tap upon our door and Ydharro entered our room. He came straight up to where we sat and counted out one hundred and fifty *reales* in silver pieces. These he laid upon the table and then turned and departed without a word of explanation or farewell!

The Basque *contrabandista* was too proud to confess his breach of faith; he was too honorable to rob me of my cash, and far too loyal to his Church to disobey the stern, distasteful command of the priest. The man's true spirit of nobleness was revealed in that silent act of repudiation and restitution, and he departed from our presence with a mingled air of pride and shame. But as he turned away he gave me a quick friendly glance and made a sign with his hand to warn us of a danger. Then he passed to the door and went out without even bidding us *adios*. And so without that familiar but sacred valediction—often so lightly given but, which, at times of final partings means so much—without that sacred farewell we parted from one another, Ydharro and I.

He failed me—and he failed me badly in the darkest hour of our need—but nonetheless I shall always remember him with admiration and pity as a perfect type of the Spanish Catholic manhood of his day—sincere, charitable, earnest and devout, but servile to the priest, and in matters of religion absolutely devoid of the spirit of independence.

Chapter 26
"Adios! Father Lorenzo"

From the window of my carefully darkened bedroom I watched Ydharro descend to stables, and in less than five minutes I saw him walk his mule across the patio and out into the road. There, by the light of the lantern that he carried, I saw him kneel in the mud and kiss the hem of Father Lorenzo's cassock and ask his blessing! Then he arose apparently with a light heart and rode swiftly away into the darkness.

Father Lorenzo now turned and walked away as if he were going to his own lodging and I went down and followed him. Up through the straggling little village he walked and up into the narrow ravine that leads to the frontier gate. Up and up he toiled slowly and silently until he approached and entered the guardroom at the gate.

I followed him as closely as I dared and then stood in the shadow just outside the guardroom door. There I heard the priest say: "*Buenas noches, Capitán!* There are three proscribed heretics at Maya who will probably attempt to pass the gate tonight before legal process can arrive for their arrest. So be on your guard and, if they present themselves, you must detain them under some pretext or other. I will come up tonight and report their movements to you. *Adios, Capitán*, and may the blessing of God abide with you."

"Amen!" said the Captain, as he accompanied the priest to the door.

Father Lorenzo now left the guardroom and began his return journey to the village–and I followed him. Near the end of the ravine he stopped at and entered a small house, and this I carefully observed and located for it was evidently the house where he lodged.

I now pursued my solitary way down the steep ravine toward the Parador Choria, and as I proceeded I became more and more despondent as I realized that here at Maya, in full sight of Protestant Navarre and at the very last stage of our long perilous journey, the probability of our escape was now even more remote than ever. The Captain of the Inquisition Guard might arrive at any moment from Urdax, which, as you remember was only five miles distant. Then, too, we were known to be lodging at the Parador Choria! Advance or retreat was now equally impossible. Our every movement was watched. Ydharro's secret track was closed to us. And here we were, at the very last hour of our desperate flight, inevitably doomed to be captured—unless. . .

But, no! The scheme that suddenly flashed to my troubled mind seemed so utterly hopeless of success. It was fraught with so many possibilities of failure! Failure through misadventure or miscalculation. It was so...But it was the *only possible means of escape* that I could devise at the moment, and, if I decided to risk it, we should have to accomplish it within the hour!

So, returning to the women, I bade them secrete the cash and valuables underneath their workmen's clothing, an abandon all else, and then come with me quickly to the priest's lodging. There, they were to wait outside in the roadway while I entered the house, and they were to wait there until I returned to them.

It was intensely dark as we entered the ravine, and it was with utmost difficulty that I managed to find the priest's residence. There, bidding the women to stand and wait in the road, I groped my way up the rock-hewn steps that led to the house, and tapped loudly and authoritatively upon the door, I inquired if Father Lorenzo was within.

"Yes," replied the old Señora of the house, in that muffled kind of voice that always betokens partial deafness—"Yes, your Excellency, the Father is, at present, upstairs in his chamber."

I thanked the Señora and, without waiting for an invitation, I walked right into the house and said: "Will you please tell him that the Captain of the Inquisition Guard is here and wishes to speak with him?"

The woman went into the back kitchen, and there shouted my message through the trapdoor that opened upstairs into the priest's bedroom.

"Tell him to come up to me" replied the priest, and thereupon, in response to Father Lorenzo's cordial invitation, I immediately ascended halfway up the ladder. Father Lorenzo opened the trap-door above my head and stood there waiting for me to ascend; but before he could recognize me or drop the trapdoor, I had roped his feet, pulled them from under him and butted him backward on the floor.

It was no time for hesitation or tenderness—or for any false ideas of sacerdotalism—three innocent lives were at stake—so I gagged him quickly, and stripped him of his long cloak, his hat and cord and crucifix, and then, having tied him securely to his bed, I bade him a final farewell.

"*Adios*, Father Lorenzo," said I. "*Adios*—Ah! So you recognize me at last, do you? YES! It is I, right enough—IT IS I, Don Fernando de la Mina! Don Fernando, whom you thought to be dead, and whose lightning-struck body you thought to have burned at your accursed Auto de Fé last October at Valladolid. *Adios*, Father Lorenzo. I am in too great a hurry to say more to you than this. I forgive you for your brutality to me, and I pray that God may bless you with a more human and Christian spirit ere you die. *Adios*, Father Lorenzo!"

The astonished and horrified priest looked at me with terror in his eyes as if he had beheld an apparition. But I dared not stay any longer with my impotent enemy. So, rolling his hat and cord and crucifix in his ample cassock, I descended with them down the ladder and securely closed the trapdoor after me. Then passing through the kitchen I entered the sitting room, and there I said to the astonished Señora: "I am very sorry to tell you, Señora, that our beloved Father Lorenzo has had a very bad fall. I fear that he must have lost his senses—he does do so sometimes. However, he is quite conscious now and, if he is un-disturbed and allowed to remain perfectly quiet for an hour or two, he will be quite well by the morning."

And after this reassuring explanation I extracted a promise from the kindly old soul that she would not disturb him herself or allow anyone else to do so.

Chapter 27

From Spain to Navarre

I then quickly rejoined the women in the Roadway, and there
I bade the Doña Rosa discard her workman's cap and don the
priest's headgear. Then I carefully drew the warm clerical cloak
over her plump shoulders and secured it round her waist with the girdle and its sacred emblem.

"Now, Señora," said I, as we began to ascend the steep ravine,
"When we come near the gate, you must go forward alone. You will
walk slowly into the guardroom and, keeping your face in the shadow,
if you can, you will say, "*Buenas noches, Capitán,* the three heretics of
whom I recently spoke to you are now riding through the village, and
will soon be coming up the ravine in the hope of making their escape
through the frontier gates. These cunning heretics are cleverly disguised as the Captain of the Inquisition Guard and two of his men. As
a priest it is impossible for me to arrest them or delay their departure
while they are still on Spanish territory and thus under civil law. But I
can and will secure these accursed Lutherans the moment they set foot
on the neutral ground that lies just outside the gate. For that purpose
I have brought with me a couple of loyal Catholics—they are following me now and will soon be here. I wish you, therefore, to instruct
your sentry to pass these two men through the gate on their giving the
password *Santiago.* Then, as soon as they have passed through, I will
follow them into the neutral territory and there we will spread our net
and capture the accursed heretics in their first glad moment of sup-
posed triumph."

Even while I was thus instructing the Doña Rosa we could already
hear the Captain of the Inquisition Guard and his horsemen advanc-

ing rapidly on us far down in the ravine below. From where we stood and right up to the Puerta the narrow ravine now rose sheer and unscalable on either side.

We were all tensely conscious that the next few moments would prove to be the climax of our anxieties. If, now, any untoward hindrance or mishap should delay us, we must inevitably be captured, for the Captain and his men would be upon us in less than five minutes time.

Doña Rosa now walked slowly forward and announced herself to the sentry as Father Lorenzo (whom in color and roundness of face and sturdy build she well resembled) and was allowed to pass into the guardroom. There we saw her speak, and speak very calmly, too, to the officer in charge. The officer, thereupon, called the two sentries to him and, to our great joy, we heard him give them the necessary instructions concerning us. Then he dismissed them back again to their respective posts.

Ana and I now advanced toward the first sentry, to be challenge.

"*Quien es?* Who goes there?" demanded the sentry.

"*Dos Cristianos*" we replied.

"Password?" he demanded.

"*Santiago,*" we replied, and thereupon the sentry permitted us to proceed toward the Puerta. Here, at the gate, we were again challenged by the second sentry, who, after receiving our replies, stepped back to the great gates and slowly opened the little wicket, through which, with hearts wildly throbbing with excitement and the joy of triumph, Ana and I passed in an instant from perils of persecuting Spain to the threshold of safety on the neutral ground!

There in the darkness just behind the wicket we now stood and waited for Doña Rosa to come through and join us. Minute after minute passed in tantalizing suspense and inactivity. We seemed to wait an interminable time–but Doña Rosa did not come! This protracted delay still further jeopardized our slender and quickly diminishing chances of escape, for while we stood there, impatient and eagerly expectant, we could hear the steady sound of approaching horsemen growing momentarily louder and louder as our inveterate foes drew near. But still Doña Rosa did not come, and we began to suffer intense agony of fear and apprehension. What if Doña Rosa's courage had failed her at the last moment under this final and terrible strain? Was it possible that the officer had detected her disguise? Had some fell accident or sudden illness incapacitated her? What was it that could so long delay her coming? Was it…?

Then presently, with startling suddenness, a thin outline of light shone round the edge of the closed wicket and, through the crevices in the thick clamped oak, we began to hear the officer questioning Doña Rosa.

"But, Father," said he to my beloved, "however do you expect that your two peasant fellows will be able to stop and capture three desperate men on horseback?"

His voice was harsh, his manner critical, and it was clear to us that, by this time, the Doña Rosa must be experiencing tremendous difficulty in maintaining her priestly and authoritative character in the face of the officer's suspicion and severe interrogation.

Happily, however, her voice, at least, did not betray her. No trepidation, hesitancy or loss of self-control was discernible in the tone of her voice as she replied firmly and slowly to the Captain's challenging question.

"By this time, *Capitán*, my two men will have fixed a loose wide net right across the neutral road, a little way beyond the Puerta." Here the officer began to cautiously open the wicket. "When the heretics arrive," she continued, "they will dismount at the Puerta so as to disarm suspicion and also in order to facilitate their escape. Then they will begin to fraternize with you and your men," bravely continued my beloved as she now drew frantically upon her untrained imagination. "Then they will wait their opportunity, or perhaps create a disturbance, and in the mêlée they will 'rush' the wicket and fly along the neutral road. But whether they pass through the Puerta peacefully or not, they will inevitably fall into our net, where they will become inextricably entangled, and my two men will then have no difficulty in overcoming and securing them one at a time.

The wicket gate was now partly opened by the officer. But he cautiously held it ajar with his arm across the opening while he deliberately protracted his interrogation of my beloved.

Through the half-open wicket we could now plainly see the Doña Rosa and the officer, for he held his lantern between them so that its light shone upon both their faces. The officer, an alert and experienced man, was now watching my beloved searchingly and critically, and I detected on his face a faint glint of suspicion. Then, as the sound of the approaching horsemen grew louder and louder, I discerned upon the Doña Rosa's countenance evidence of a glowing and increasing fearfulness which, I foresaw, would inevitably betray us unless I could at once support my beloved in her tragic acting. So, bending my head beneath the officer's outstretched arm, I stepped briskly and confidently through the wicket and stood between the lamp and my beloved so that a deep shadow was thrown over her face. Then, looking reassuringly at her I said; "Father, I find that we shall require the use of a lantern for a few moments. Do you think the officer would kindly lend us his?"

This unexpected and timely diversion immediately restored the Doña Rosa's confidence and at the same time it served to disconcert the officer, who being thus momentarily taken off his guard, now turned his attention exclusively to me. I thereupon stretched out my hand for the lamp with an expectant gesture—a gesture to which he involuntarily responded with instinctive courtesy and handed me his lantern.

No sooner had he done this, however, then he suddenly recovered his suspicion and reached out his hand for its return, saying, with an authoritative air as he opened the wicket, "I will go through into the neutral ground with you."

Seeming not to notice the gesture that he made for the return of the lamp, but at the same time discreetly appearing to comply with the resolve to accompany us, I now drew the Doña Rosa close to me and, pushing her toward the wicket, I whispered, "Go through first." Then, still holding the light, I slowly followed her through; but, as I stepped across the iron-clamped bar that was fixed beneath the wicket, I turned the light courteously toward the officer so as to enable him to follow us, but as I turned to do so we were all suddenly plunged into darkness—because I stumbled and trod upon the lantern!

What happened after that, on the Spanish side of the gate I really do not know—all was confusion and excitement. But, immediately after I had extinguished the lamp, a sudden roar arose in the darkness. A savage roar that rose from the ravine. "Stop those heretics! Stop those heretics," shouted the Captain of the Inquisition Guard, who was now only a few hundred yards away. "Stop those heretics!" he shouted as he and his men rode madly toward the gate.

"Password!" shouted the sentry.

"Password be cursed!" roared the Captain of the Inquisition Guard.

Then there was loud talking and mutual recriminations, in which the sentries, the officer, and the Captain all joined, but which we dared not stay to hear; but, taking the women's hands in mine, I fled with them for dear life across the narrow strip of neutral ground, and rushing us to the Navarrois sentry I shouted: "We are persecuted Protestants of Spain, and we come to crave the protection of Her Majesty the Queen of Navarre."

The Navarrois sentry commanded us to stand. He held his lantern to our faces and then bade us precede him into the guardroom.

There, seated at the table, was the Captain of the Navarrois Guard, who looked up from the papers that he was examining and scanned us critically. Then he demanded our names, rank, and present purpose.

In response to this inquiry, I stepped forward and laid Detreño's receipt before him upon the table and said:

"*Monsieur le Capitaine*, I am Pablo Acedo, a Protestant merchant of Tolosa in Spain, and I have escaped from the prison of the Inquisition at Valladolid. In company with that lady"–and here I pointed to the Doña Rosa and signaled her to cast off Father Lorenzo's cloak and hat–"that lady," I continued, "who, though disguised just now as a priest and even now as a workman, is in reality the Doña Rosa de Riello of Simancas, and this other workman is Ana Cabaña, her maid. We have come to crave the protection of her Majesty Queen Jeanne, and the hospitality of her generous subjects. *Monsieur le Capitaine*, we crave your protection and we place our lives in your keeping."

The Captain remained impassive throughout my appeal and then replied coldly and officially: "If your statement is true, you may be sure of protection, but until our courts are satisfied I shall have to hold you as prisoners of Navarre." Then, calling to his orderly, he said, "Conduct these prisoners to the cell and give them light, food, and blankets."

I thanked the Captain for his consideration, but he received my gratitude stoically and then took no further heed to us until the guard-room door was suddenly flung wide open and the burly Captain of the Spanish Inquisition Guard burst furiously into our presence and shouted madly to the Captain of the Navarrois Guard: "In the name of His Most Catholic Majesty, King Phillip of Spain, I demand the surrender of those three escaped heretics!" Then, stepping manfully across the room, he seized the Doña Rosa and then pushed Ana and me before him toward the door.

"**Stand!**" shouted the Navarrois Captain. "His Majesty the King of Spain has no jurisdiction here. These prisoners are mine, and they shall remain in my care. Captain, your religious zeal has outstepped your discretion and your courtesy. Stand, I say! **Stand I say!**" repeated the angry and indignant Protestant Captain as, ringing his loud table

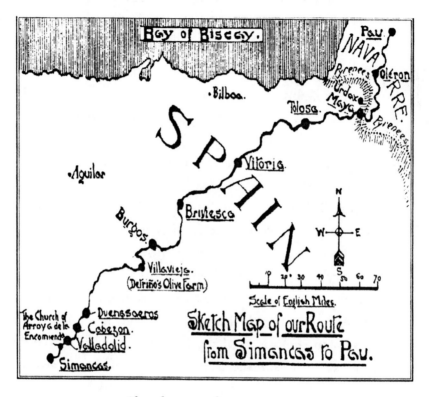

Sketch map of escape route.

bell, he brought two armed sentries rushing into the doorway.

With a quick but generous revulsion of feeling the Catholic Captain stood still under the Navarrois' just rebuke. Then, realizing his impotency, and his error, he apologized for his indiscretion, bade the Protestant Captain "Good night," and passed out away into the darkness toward the Puerta de Mayo, and we saw him no more.

Chapter 28
The Dawn of a Brighter Day

My son, I have now nearly reached the end of this eventful history, but I will not yet lay down my pen because I still have many details of our succeeding joys and alas, one great horror to relate to you.

Some of these, my son, I know you delight to hear, and the one great horror that I shall be constrained to record will certainly revolt you. But it is well that you should read it; and I would that not only you but that every other Protestant should read it and–remember!

But, for the moment, I must now return to the first day of our liberty. "**Liberty**" did I say–Well! On that first glad day we certainly deemed ourselves free–and indeed we were free from persecution and the fear of death. But paradoxically enough, our first night of "liberty" was spent in the prison of the Navarrois guardroom, and the next morning saw us dismissed from the prison under an armed escort upon a fifty-mile journey in order to undergo our trial at Pau, the capital of Navarre. But comfortable lodgings *en route*, the exhilarating mountain air, and the exercise and good food, soon refreshed our health and spirits, and already, early on our way, we began to anticipate the real joys of liberty. We traveled nearly thirty miles on that first day of our journey and, in the evening, when we were still about twenty miles from our destination, we were installed in good quarters at the Parador Erreguinña (the Queen's Inn) at Oléron.

There, after supper, I said to your mother: "Señora, tomorrow will secure freedom for us all and after then you will have no further need of protection. Therefore, my beloved mistress, tomorrow your servant will bid you farewell."

Your mother looked wistfully at me as I spoke these words, and I could see—and I was glad to see—that she dreaded the implied separation. Tears glistened in her eyes as with trembling lips she replied: "I do not desire you to leave us. We are, as you know, women with no experience of the foreign land into which we have now come, and we shall need your protection more than ever. Can you not remain with us?"

"You are fatigued, Señora," I replied. "Seek your rest and we will talk about our future plans tomorrow. *Buenas noches,* Señora, and may the blessing of God abide with you."

Early next morning your mother and Ana descended to the common room in the feminine attire that they had purchased in the town, and, after breakfast, I asked them to come to my room and bring to me the Doña Rosa's money and jewelry. These I spread out upon my bed so that your mother might count and receive them.

A strained feeling now possessed us all as, for the first time, we stood together unobserved in conscious safety. We had passed through so many perils together. Perils that had united us in sympathy, loyalty, and unquestioning confidence in one another. And now this bond of true and tested friendship that we had woven with so much suffering and anxiety was about to be dissolved and lost in our forthcoming freedom. The very liberty that we had all striven so hard to win was destined now to separate us forever. Your mother was the first to speak.

She said: "Señor, I deeply regret that you desire to leave me. You have been more than a servant to me. You have been a noble and unselfish friend. Must you go? I do not desire to inquire into your prospects—indeed, I do not know who you really are! But you know who I am, and you know that my destination is Paris, where one of Don Fernando's cousins lives. There I shall have a home and protection, but..."—and here her tears began to peep again and her color came and went—"I shall have a home and protection, yes, but I shall never enjoy the happiness that gladdened my girlhood and promised me such joy in life."

Ana, dear soul, soothed and comforted her, and then she resumed: "You have preserved for me my life and all the wealth I now possess, and I know that you have only a few gold pieces. I cannot detain you if you wish to leave me, but, before you depart, I must ask your acceptance–not of a reward for your courage and kindness, that would be impossible–but just a souvenir of our brief and never, never-to-be-forgotten companionship in peril. There lie before you all the money and precious things that I possess. Take from them just what you will. They are mine to give, thanks to your wisdom and bravery. What will you accept?"

"I can accept nothing, Señora," I replied, "for the only gift that I crave is one that I fear you will never give me."

Chapter 29
I Plead for Recognition

She misunderstood my intent and colored deeply with embarrassment. But I, disregarding her mistaken indignation, reached over to the jewels that lay spread out upon the bed, and took from among them a small diamond and ruby ring–the ring that I had given her upon our betrothal three years ago and said: "This is the only souvenir I crave, Señora."

Then I pressed the tiny ring upon my little finger and slowly turned it round so that it should appear like a man's wedding ring, and as I did so, I looked laughingly at her just as I used to do when I teased her in the old happy days at Simancas. My voice, my gestures and my looks all betrayed me, for I was now careless–nay, desirous–of discovery. But even then, incredulous as it may seem, the women did not, or would not, realize my identity, so sure had they and the whole world been of my decease three weeks ago in the Church of Arroya de la Encomienda and the burning of my lightning-struck body at the Auto de Fé on the following Sunday!

"No! No, Señor," replied my beloved. "I could not part with that little ring. It is my betrothal ring, and it is dearer to me than life. But do not refuse to take any other jewel as a souvenir, and also please take from me as much money as you need. Remember that you will have to start life again amid all the difficulties and racial prejudices of a foreign land, for you can never return to Spain, because there you have made yourself an outlaw for my sake and for my sake alone."

"Not exactly so," I interrupted, "for, as I told you, I, too, fell under the ban of the Church of Spain six months before you honored me with your employ."

And here again, by that strange inconsistency of a sensitive woman, your beloved mother began to weep afresh. Perhaps it was the prospect of our parting and the fell foreboding of loneliness that distressed her.

For a while I stood and waited for the passion of grief to pass, and then I said: "Señora, you are young–a long future lies before you. I pray you look forward with hopefulness and joy and believe with me that the darkness of the recent hour was but the prelude of a brighter day."

"Señor," she replied tearfully, "it is even now as I told you in the Plazuela del Hospicio. The light has gone out from my earthly life–the dead do not return."

"But suppose," said I, "suppose...You know that Don Fernando escaped from prison to the Church of Arroya de la Encomienda, and you and all the world believe that the officers of the Inquisition found him there dead and disfigured by lightning. But, Señora, you know, too, that when the officers arrived there they found or thought they found–a poor ragged *buhonero* standing in the church alive and well beside the dead body of Don Fernando. But suppose, Señora, suppose that when he entered the church he had found there awaiting him the dead and disfigured body of a poor *buhonero*; and suppose that, discerning in this dreadful circumstance the Providence of God, Don Fernando had quickly changed his own gay attire for the rags of that dead *buhonero*. Suppose, too, that on the morrow, contrary to what the whole world believes, suppose that Don Fernando, disguised in the peddler's rags, had witnessed the fires of the Auto de Fé consume the gaily attired body of the poor stricken *buhonero* instead of his own! And suppose, too, that, knowing now that the flames had finally destroyed all evidence of the truth, suppose that Don Fernando had restarted life as Timoteo Pereño the *buhonero*, and had resolutely determined to reveal his secret to none save his betrothed, and then not until he had escaped with her to a land of safety!

118

Suppose it was he who at the Plazuela del Hospicio claimed, by his certain knowledge, to foresee your future and out of that certain knowledge had bid you believe that the darkness of that present hour was but the prelude of a brighter day! Suppose it was he who, fearing that you intended to escape from his protecting care at Valladolid, had bribed the treacherous ostler and had followed and rescued you from arrest near Cabezón! Suppose it was he whose mysterious knowledge of the French language had bewildered you so when he detected the cunning of Father Lorenzo at Dueñasaeros. Suppose it was he who had saved you from that crafty priest in our little oil store at Burgos. No servant and no other earthly friend than he who loves you would have thus risked the flames for you."

Then, harking back to things and thoughts that she and I had shared long years ago—secrets that she and I alone could know—I asked: "Señora, do you remember, when you were a little girl, and so proud a little girl in your silver-trimmed blue velvet gown, do you remember how you cried because Don Fernando kissed your cousin Mirienda? Do you remember that once, when you and he were quite alone at the Castillete de Riello—it was the first of June, and your sixteenth birthday—do you remember that, as you and he stood together under the fig tree in the patio, Don Fernando took your hand and kissed it, and, because you smiled, he kissed your lips? Have you forgotten that warm embrace of glowing youth that sealed the declaration of his love? Do you remember when, three years ago last May, Don Fernando pressed this little ring upon your finger and vowed to love and honour you forever? Do you remember—do you think you will ever forget—those tender words you gave him in reply: '*Fernando mio*, I have always loved you. I love you more dearly than my life!' Do you remember the words that Fernando whispered in your ear? *I do!*"

Chapter 30

"Rosa, Roseta Hermosa Mia"

My beloved was very quiet all the while I spoke. Ana had stepped back to the window so that she should not overhear the last part of my appeal.

My beloved was very quiet; she did not move or seem to listen. Then, looking down upon the floor, she said:

"Ever since you spoke to me in the Plazuela del Hospicio I have suspected this—but I have never dared to believe it, lest it should prove false—I did so dread a disillusion! Yet right through those dreadful days I have always been conscious of the nearness of a loving power and my hope has been continually sustained by the influence of your presence. Sometimes, when I have searched your face and seen you smile, and sometimes when I heard your merry laugh and your seemingly familiar voice, sometimes I allowed myself to half believe that you were he. And yet I could not see how that could be, for everybody knew that you were dead.

And then, and then, as I allowed these seeming certainties to contradict my hopes, the cruel certainty of your death would gradually triumph and banish all my hopes and leave me more lonely and desolate than ever. When, at Detriño's olive farm, you pretended that I was your wife, and when, next day at Burgos, you twitted me so knavishly about the furnishing of our home, I heard and recognized a joyous echo of our far-off merriment of old. And when, later, too, as a weak and unhappy woman, I craved the comfort of the Confessional, and you so firmly thwarted my folly and then so reverently and sincerely reconfirmed my reasonable faith, then I seemed to realize the impact of your loving wisdom and sound judgment on my soul. I felt that my loved one spoke again to me through you and that, through your human agency, the spirit of Don Fernando de la Mina had returned to safeguard my earthly happiness and my eternal hope. But even then, throughout all our recent close and intimate association, I always feared—even as I fear it now—that these transient respites from despair will prove to be nothing but a dream—a dream from which I shall wake again to a bitter disappointment and a life-long loneliness." And she wept silently.

Tenderly I drew near to her and, kneeling, held her little hand in mine, just as I used to do in our golden days of happy love, and then, looking up in to her bewildered face, I whispered:

"*Confia, confia, Rosa mia!*" Rejoice, my little one, that in God's gracious Providence the dead do sometimes return. The precious life and love you deemed for ever lost is now restored to you, purified and strengthened by suffering and danger. *Confia, cofia, Rosa mia*, and let your dead hopes rise again into a happier and holier gladness, for we have passed together through the night of horror and now, by the mercy and the love of God, we have come in safety to the joyous dawn of a brighter and happier day. *Rosa, Roseta Hermosa mia*, give me this little ring that I may return it to you as a sacred emblem of my plighted troth and as a souvenir of the sorrows through which we have passed and as an earnest of the happiness that, in God's continued love, shall yet be ours. *Rosa mia. . .*"

There was a preemptory knock at the door, and the younger of the two soldiers who were escorting us as prisoners to Pau announced that the horses were ready and that we must start away at once.

Chapter 31

In Prison at Pau

A cold mist rolled down from the mountains and obscured the cheerless landscape as your mother and I rode merrily side by side, talking joyfully to one another in the sweet, old, familiar way, just as if no dreadful interlude had ever come between us to divide our happy intercourse. We talked, too, with sadness, of our dear old homes and of the days that were now passed from us forever. And then we began to talk more joyously about our hopes and prospects in the unknown future. We realized that we should now have to start a new life—a new life in such different circumstances from those we had expected. No fortune, no family estates, no nationality, no status of nobility, and not a single friend near to us in the whole wide world save our dear old faithful Ana.

But we were happy, supremely happy, for our happiness was founded, not on the shifting and deceptive sands of fortune, but upon love that had been tried in the severest adversity—a love that had been strengthened and deepened by sorrow and proved by mutual faithfulness.

We were poor, negligible folk, but we were *free* and *young* and *brave*, and therefore the whole world lay at our feet before us. So throughout that dismal day, prisoners though we were, we rode on merrily through the mud and the rain, chatting as cheerily as children. On we pressed till evening, when the sky began to clear and the setting sun lit fires on the rosy peaks of the distant Pyrénées, and tinted with a golden glow the gray Palace of Pau that now loomed ahead of us, poised picturesquely upon its deep cleft rock.

We rode across the bridge into the castle enclosure, and there we dismounted and were led to our prison cells in the further tower, there to await our summons to answer the charges against us in the adjoining Courts of Justice.

A little while before noon next day we were arraigned in the council chamber as "Criminals escaped from Spain—aliens who had entered Navarre without permit, business or authority." The charge was true, but before sentence could be passed upon us I begged permission to address the court. Permission being granted me to speak, I boldly addressed the presiding justices, and told them of our status of nobility in Spain and of the religious persecution that had driven us to escape from our native land. I also pleaded that, for our future safety, our names and the details of our escape should be revealed only to Her Majesty the Queen.

Such a request was unprecedented in Navarre, but the sincerity of my appeal won the consideration of the justices, and we were commanded to appear next morning in the royal audience chamber.

Early next morning I dressed myself very carefully. I also bade your mother select and wear her most beautiful jewels, for I anticipated that the Queen, who had once loved that handsome trifler Antoine L'Echangeur, whom she had made a king, would not be insensible to the grace and beauty of a daintily attired Spanish gentlewoman. Nor was she, for, as we entered the royal presence, I was conscious that the Queen was deeply impressed by the winsome loveliness of my bride-to-be.

We made our obeisance to Her Majesty, and were commanded by the Chancellor Nicolas to draw near to present our petition. I told the Protestant Queen of my arraignment, torture and flight, and of the confiscation of our estates, and I prayed that Her Majesty would grant us protection and permission to proceed from Navarre to our friends at Paris.

"For this permission," replied the Queen, "you must patiently abide the decision of my councilors, but have no fear for your safety, for the vengeance of Rome has no power in my realm. Prisoners of Navarre receive justice and the disciples of the Reformed Faith have liberty of conscience and protection."

With that gracious assurance our audience terminated, and we were then conducted back to our cells to await the confirmation of our statements and the decision of the courts.

Chapter 32
Art Triumphs Over Diplomacy

During the three or four months of our continued imprisonment I beguiled my leisure by designing new patterns of choice embroidery for the embellishment of our future home. As a child I was blessed with an inherited capacity to enjoy beautiful things and also with some power to create new schemes in form and color. In the new patterns that I now produced I blended the rich colorings of the old Hispaño-Morisco fabrics (which I know so well) with the chaste and noble forms of the new art of Italy, and your mother and Ana wrought my abstract designs into a glorious reality in the form of tapestries and hangings for cushions, bed furniture and window draperies. Now it so happened that the wardress who attended your mother and Ana became keenly interested in these beautiful things, and her admiration was communicated to the jailer, and from him to the household servants, and from them to the Court and the Queen. And one day, early in the spring of 1560, Her Majesty commanded your mother and me to bring some specimen of our handiwork to the Queens's small chamber for the royal inspection.

When the Queen saw our artistic handiwork she was greatly charmed with it and graciously expressed her appreciation. Indeed her admiration was so well-informed and so generous that your mother craved Her Majesty's acceptance of all or any of the pieces. Queen Jeanne graciously selected a small but very rich panel of tapestry that was wrought in cherry-red, gold and verdigris green, and she announced her intention of sending this piece as a present to the Queen Regent of France, Catherine of Medici. This she did, and in the following summer the Queen of France replied to Queen Jeanne, and, returned thanks for the panel of tapestry. She added to her acknowledgment a gracious request that the artists who had produced such original and beautiful workmanship should be invited to visit Paris and enter the service of the French Queen for at least one year.

This royal request at once secured our liberty, and in the summer of 1560 your mother and I received our Royal and kindly *congé* and started on our journey to Paris. After nearly two months of leisurely traveling, we duly arrived at the French Capital and there we were received into the Palais de Conde, in the Rue de Grenelle, by my cousin, Don Reitto de la Mina. My cousin was then the private and confidential secretary to the Protestant Prince of Conde, who was brother-in-law to the Queen of Navarre. There, at the Hôtel Condé, in Paris, we three all worked happily together: I creating my designs and your mother and Ana, with her French maids, interpreting them into embroideries and tapestries for the embellishment of the new Palace of the Tuilleries that was then being designed by the architects. Our work was congenial and was much appreciated. The Queen Regent' payments to us were prompt and liberal, and we soon began to accumulate the real nucleus of our present wealth.

One thing alone spoiled the completeness of our happiness. Nearly two years had now passed since the day that your mother and I had so fondly hoped would be our wedding day, and yet here we were robbed of our estates, degraded from our proud position, banished for ever from our native land, and now mere aliens. Yes! aliens, and mere dependents in an alien land for, though we were living in a palace, we were absolutely dependent for our very lives and livelihood upon the protection and patronage of a foreign sovereign and a Catholic!

Early in the following May, however, Queen Catherine of Medici gave her gracious consent to our marriage, and on May 18th, 1561, just two years later than we had once so fondly hoped, Don Fernando de la Mina, Embroiderer to Her Majesty the Queen Regent of France, was married at the Protestant Church in the Rue de Grenelle at Paris to Doña Rosa de Riello, in the presence of the Prince of Condé and my cousin, Don Rietto de la Mina.

Chapter 33
The Massacre on St. Bartholomew's Day

Our happiness was now nearly complete, I say "nearly," because the happiest and the holiest consummation of our joy was not fully reached until the following March, when your mother and I were blessed by God's supremest gift to us—a healthful, happy little son, a true expression of our mutual love. A bonny boy endowed with the beauty of his mother and the merry and vivacious spirit of his father. Henceforth, our dearest care and mutual hopes were now centered in you, my son, and the days and years passed peacefully away as we watched you grow in strength and gracefulness.

But, in the larger world outside our own happy little family circle, there seethed around us hatred, treachery, religious wars and oppressive tyranny—for the people of France were, at that time, unhappily divided into two opposing camps and divided, too, by the worst kind of division that can ever separate a nation or a society—they were divided by an irreconcilable religious disagreement. Consequently, religious antipathies ran high in those distressful days in France. Hatred—bitter, mutual hatred persisted between the Protestants and the Roman Catholics—and this hatred was fomented and cunningly exploited by the scheming and unscrupulous politicians of the day, for their own ambitious and unworthy ends. And, my son, believe me—the chief of those unscrupulous politicians was none other than Catherine—the Queen Regent herself! She was a stern, proud ambitious woman and cared little or nothing for religion—save as a means of achieving her political ends—and so, having failed to overthrow the Protestant cause in straight forward open warfare, she now resolved to destroy it and rid it from her realm by treachery and stealthy wholesale murder!! To this end she cat-pawed her Catholic subjects, and in-flamed their hatred. Indeed, so skillfully did she incite their cunning and their cruelty that, though she herself did not personally injure a single soul, yet she was (and she boasted that she was) instrumental in effecting the murder of no less than 70,000 of her innocent Protestant subjects during the Massacre of St. Bartholomew's Day!

That wholesale massacre was a horror—an unspeakable horror—and it was perpetrated by the Queen and those in high Roman Catholic Authority with a fiendish brutality that has no parallel in history save, perhaps, that of Nero!

And yet, my son, so far as I, a self proclaimed Protestant, was personally concerned, Queen Catherine was both generous and indulgent. In token of this I must tell you that, early in 1572 when you were just ten years old, the Queen very considerately removed us from our cramped quarters in the Palais de Condé to a much more comfortable apartment in the Palace of the Louvre. There in our lodging in the uppermost floor, we continued to produce our choice embroidery in close company with several other artists and skilled artificers who, like ourselves, were also lodged where while making various things of beauty for the new Palace of the Tuilleries.

Among these fellow artists were Jean Bréssueil—a metal worker and a Roman Catholic; Alphonse Montennier—a carver in ivory—also a Roman Catholic; and Messer Bernard Palissy—a Huguenot (as the Protestants are called in France) and he, like ourselves, was a fervent member of the Reformed Church.

Palissy and I were staunch friends—as all Protestants ought to be. At that time, he was just fifty-three years of age and thus fifteen years my senior—but he always seemed to me to be much older than that because of his sober-mindedness and his contemplative disposition. About seventeen years previous to our meeting one another, Palissy, by dint of much study and research, had discovered the secret of producing white enamel pottery, and of applying modeled fruit and fishes, etc., to ornament the surface of his glazed paste. His pottery was most exquisite and he alone was the unique artificer of this glazed and decorated faïence. In consequence of his supreme talent and service—Hugenot though he was—he enjoyed the secure protection and patronage of the powerful Queen Regent and her feeble, weak-willed son, King Charles IX.

Early in August 1572, great preparations were being made in Paris for the celebration of the forthcoming Royal and very popular wedding—a wedding that had been most cunningly and skillfully brought about by the Queen Mother—between the protestant Prince Henry of Béarn (son of my late protectress, the Queen of Navarre) and the Roman Catholic Princess, Margaret de Valois, the Daughter of Queen Catherine and sister to the reigning King Charles IX.

The prospect of this seemingly auspicious, peace-provoking wedding completely lulled the religious and political fears and apprehensions of the Huguenots—as the subtle Queen intended it should—and the result was that many of the most eminent of the Reformed Church folk and also vast crowds of ordinary Protestants were, thereby, lured to Paris. Then, just when Paris was crowded with her religious enemies—invited as friends—the Queen secretly assembled her most influential Catholic partisans in Council, and there matured and explained her long-contemplated plot to massacre every Huguenot in France!

Such was the hatred that was fomented by the Queen and her highly-placed Catholic counselors that they were easily able to enlist into their army of murderers hundreds of religious fanatics in Paris alone. Fanatics who were willing and eager to execute the awful will of their brutally bigoted Queen! The date of the massacre was duly fixed by the Queen and her Council; and numerous murderers were appointed in the various districts of the city—and the secret midnight signal was agreed upon!

But not every Protestant in Paris was foredoomed to slaughter in that night of horror. There were several favoured Protestants who were especially exempted—but they were not exempted from motives of kindness or humanity. O! No, NO! For instance, as in the case of Palissy and myself, and perhaps several others like us—we were privileged only because of our unique service to the Queen—and even then we were not exempted until after the most alluring persuasion, and then the most terrible threats had failed to make us renounce our Faith. Why, even so late as the morning of the massacre (of which we had not the least suspicion or reason for expecting) even so late as the morning of the 24th of August the Queen Mother and King Charles IX, came into the large attic studio which Palissy and I shared and there, after receiving our obeisance and inspecting our work; the young King awkwardly approached Palissy, the potter, and said to him:

"Palissy, circumstances have arisen that make it necessary for me to tell you that unless you renounce your heresy and attend Mass today, I shall be unable to protect you any longer, and I shall, therefore, be compelled . . ."

"Compelled! Your Majesty," interrupted Palissy with calm surprise. "Compelled, did you say? That is a strange word to hear from the lips of a King!" "Compelled! Permit me," continued my sincere and courageous *confrère*. "Permit me to assure Your Majesty, that there is no power that can **compel** a Potter to kneel before an image of clay!"

My son, I heard Palissy, the potter, say those very words to King Charles IX of France! And, as he spoke them, I was astounded and exhilarated by my friend's staunchness and temerity. But, the King, on hearing and seeing Palissy's determination, turned angrily and followed his forceful Mother sullenly out of the studio.

Now, strangely enough, throughout that day, every exit from the Palace was closed to us and we began to realize that we were being forcibly detained like prisoners, and we wondered why! Now, it so happened, my son, that, at that time you were not very well—just a childish sickness and, therefore, your mother kept you in bed in your little room at the back of the studio. There, quite late in the night, she continued to sit by your bedside—very likely you remember it now!

Throughout that day—and especially toward the evening—there was a strange sense of uneasiness in the Palace and, we ourselves, experienced the feeling of a dread foreboding. Palissy and I stood and looked from our studio window down into the streets of Paris that evening and, as we looked, they seemed to us to be unusually quiet as if the city were waiting for some grim happening! Late into the night we stood there, Palissy and I, watching the traffic grow less and less, as the streets become more and more deserted. The lights in the houses were extinguished one by one as the unsuspecting inhabitants retired to their rest, and presently all Paris seemed to be wrapped in peaceful slumber. It was very nearly midnight.

"What's that?" suddenly asked my companion, as he drew back from the window in sudden alarm—"What's that?"

"It's the Palace Bell," I replied—and the words were no sooner out of my mouth than the echoing tocsin rang out from the Tower of St. Germaine l'Auxerrois nerby—it was the murderous Council's Signal for the Assassins to begin their Butchery! Instantly and eagerly, in answer to that awful summons, half a dozen ruffians rushed into the quiet street that lay below on the east side of the Louvre, and there they collected at the door of one of the houses immediately opposite our side of the Palace. There, under the direction of their leader, they hammered with their bludgeons on the panels of the door and demanded admission. Messer Beronnier, the owner and occupier of the house—a wealthy Protestant merchant, kindly and loyal—opened an upper window, and, in turn, demanded to know why he had been disturbed in this unseemly way! The crowd below howled and answered him with ridicule and abuse—bidding the "heretic" descend and admit them to the house.

Messer Beronnier closed the window, and the crowd waited a few moments. Then, losing their patience, they burst in the door and rushed up the stairs into the house. Presently they all descended again and returned to the street dragging their helpless victim with them, and there, in the street, they brutally clubbed and stabbed him to death! Then Madame was brought down and dragged into the street where, shrieking amid the rough laughter and the blasphemy, she, too, was done to death. Then the two grown sons and three small children and the maid were all brought out and brutally slaughtered, and their bodies flung in a bleeding heap in front of the house!! Then, with brutal yells and laughter, the ruffians passed on to their next insensate orgies of butchery, three doors and then seven doors away. And so, in a hundred different parts of Paris, the Massacre of St. Bartholomew's Day began and continued throughout that night of horror!

I have heard it said that on that fatal night nearly every street in Paris ran red with blood! That, of course, was an exaggeration. But, long before the massacre ceased, I saw the gully in the roadway, opposite the King's Palace, thick with a turgid stream of innocent Protestant blood that flowed from the several heaps of dead that lay strewn along the foot path. It was computed that no less than ten thousand Protestants perished in Paris alone, on that dreadful night; and afterwards, at the Queen's command and with the King's consent the massacre was extended to nearly every town and village in France where no less than seventy thousand innocent people perished at the behest of the Queen and the Roman Catholic Authorities.

Yes! My son, facts are stubborn things, and the proved, historic facts of the Auto de Fé in Spain and the Massacre of St. Bartholomew's Day in France, both of which I witnessed, cannot be easily explained away by Jesuistical arguments. Neither can they be excused or extenuated in the light of the simple and uncontaminated teaching and example of Jesus Christ!—But be this as it may, however, the self-styled "Vicar of Christ on Earth" actually exulted in the Massacre of St. Bartholomew's Day, and he even applauded the perpetrators of the dreadful deed for the religious zeal that they evinced in such unspeakable

St. Bartholomew's Day massacre.

brutality. His "Holiness" the Pope of Rome so far rejoiced in the Massacre that he celebrated the "Triumph," as he called it, by a grand Te Deum, and by the proclamation of a Year of Jubliee; and, I am told, too, that his "Holiness" has caused a medal to be struck in commemoration of this horror!

Rome boast that she never changes—Let Protestants Beware!

Chapter 34
The Land of Religious Liberty

My son, I am now drawing toward the close of this eventful history. You will remember, perhaps, how alarmed and distressed we were at the massacre of our friends and co-religionists in Paris, and how apprehensive we became for our own future safety. And you will, I know, remember how in the following autumn we suddenly and secretly left Paris and fled—disguised—to la Rochelle, whence we escaped in an English merchant ship to Plymouth and from thence sailed to London. And you will, I am sure, always remember with grateful pleasure the warm welcome we received in London at the hands of my boyhood chum, Simeon Levi, the Jewish Banker of Lombard Street. Simeon and I had been staunch chums in our old days at Simancas, and he and I had been partners there in many a daring escapade. It was he whom I accompanied in Toledo in 1556 in our successful search for the long-lost treasure of his ancestor, Samuel Levi, the Philanthropist and Banker of Toledo, and Treasurer of State to Don Pedro "the Cruel" who foully murdered him for his wealth.

Simeon Levi, as you know is very rich—and very generous, and it was largely due to his magnanimous gift (for he would not allow it to be *loan*)—it was due to Simeon's gift that we were able to take up our residence and make our comfortable home and our business quarters at the sign of "The Golden Cross" on Cornhill. Thanks also to the influence of young Sir Philip Sydney (whom I had know in Paris), I was very soon appointed "Embroiderer to Her Majesty, Queen Elizabeth III," and by far the most gracious Queen whom it has been my proud privilege to serve.

You remember, too, how in the summer of 1588 when the proud Armada approached the free and hospitable shores of Britain my heart was torn between a natural love of my native land and a well-merited hatred of Spanish tyranny and religious intolerance. You remember how the arrogant threat of the King of Spain and the Divinely ordered destruction of his fleet completely killed forever in my heart the last lingering affection for my native land.

Well, My son, the end of my history draws near, and I desire to conclude it with a pen of thanksgiving to Almighty God for His long continued mercy to me and mine. For, under His infinite wisdom and love I was led as a youth into the Light; then, in the pride of early manhood, I was humbled by the Powers of Darkness. I have experienced the pangs of suffering and death, and I have experienced the sweetness of reprieve, the joy of life and the unspeakable happiness of requited love. I have suffered poverty and hardship, but through it all I have enjoyed the sanctifying consciousness of the Divine Providence. I have tasted the joy of liberty after imprisonment, prosperity after privation, and perfect love after loneliness and persecution. And now, as my day declines, I thank God for having spared me and mine through so many dangers and vicissitudes of fortune. I thank Him for having blessed your mother and me with wealth, honour and happiness in a ripe and healthful old age. I thank Him for His gift of you, my son, and for all the joy that you have brought us, and I thank Him for dear old Ana's loyalty and love.

And now I bequeath to you our wealth and our name—a name that has never been dishonored; and I will reveal to you now, for the first time, the proud and quaint old motto of our race, "*El Papa, el Rey, y yo.* The Pope, the King and I." But here let me urge you never to forget that this proud family motto, together with our ancient heritage and our age-long claim to Spanish nobility, were once and forever surrendered by me at the Church of Arroya de la Encomienda on that October afternoon more than forty years ago, when in the Providence of God I accepted the rags of a *buhonero* and his poverty and ignominy in exchange for the glorious gift of life with all its unknown future possibilities. And now, out of the experience of my years, I bequeath to you a worthier motto to inscribe beneath our crest: "*Amad la fraternidad. Temed á Dios. Honrad al rey.* Love the Brotherhood. Fear God. Honour the King."

"Farewell, my beloved son, until we meet you in Heaven."

—Fernando de la Mina

Given this 14th day of September, in the Year of Our Lord, 1601, at the Sign of "The Golden Cross" on Cornhill, in the City of London